The Falconer Files
Book
by
Andrea Frazer

The Falconer Files Brief Cases
Books 1 - 4
Andrea Frazer
This edition published by JDI Publications 2024
Copyright 2013 by Andrea Frazer

Other books by Andrea Frazer

The Belchester Chronicles

Strangeways to Oldham

White Christmas with a Wobbly Knee

Snowballs and Scotch Mist

Old Moorhen's Shredded Sporran

Caribbean Sunset with a Yellow Parrot

God Rob Ye Merry Gentlemen

The Falconer Files

Death of an Old Git

Choked Off

Inkier than the Sword

Pascal Passion

Murder at the Manse

Music to Die For

Strict and Peculiar

Christmas Mourning

Grave Stones

Death in High Circles

Glass House

Bells and Smells

Shadows and Sins

Nuptial Sacrifice

The Fine Line

High Wired

Tightrope

Holmes and Garden

The Curious Case of the Black Swansong

The Bookcase of Sherman Holmes

Other Titles

Choral Mayhem

Down and Dirty in the Dordogne

1

ANDREA FRAZER

A Fresh of Breath Air

Author's note

Brief Cases is an occasional series of short stories, used as a device to record the times between the full-length works of The Falconer Files. They confirm that life does go on in the meantime, between big cases, and that not everything they work on together is of the highest priority. I hope you enjoy reading them as much as I have enjoyed writing them.

The books in this collection

Book 1. Love Me To Death

On Christmas Day the two detectives are summoned to a block of apartments in Market Darley, to investigate the unexplained death of a young woman whose fiancé was due to move in with her on New Year's Day.

At first, her death seems a complete mystery, then, something that Dr Christmas discovers on the internet indicates that her death could just have been a tragic accident, or was it?

Book 2. A Sidecar Named Expire

A young man and his girlfriend decide to celebrate their first St Valentine's Day together, with a cosy evening of cocktails at her house. But as the evening progresses, events don't go quite as Malcolm Standing planned.

The next morning, DI Falconer and DS Carmichael are called in to try to sort out what really happened.

Book 3. Battered To Death

DI Falconer and DS Carmichael are both enjoying a well-earned rest day, when they are summoned to a most distressing incident that has occurred at a chip shop on the parade of shops in Upper Darley.

It was obviously murder, but was it something to do with the robust behaviour of some of the more aggressive customers from the night before or was it closer to home?

Book 4. Toxic Gossip

DI Falconer becomes involved in a gossip-fuelled hate crime, only to find himself questioning his own judgement when it comes to protecting Miriam Darling from her anonymous persecutors...

Love Me To Death

On Christmas Day the two detectives are summoned to a block of apartments in Market Darley, to investigate the unexplained death of a young woman whose fiancé was due to move in with her on New Year's Day.

At first, her death seems a complete mystery, then, something that Dr Christmas discovers on the internet indicates that her death could just have been a tragic accident, or was it?

CHRISTMAS 2009

STAVE ONE

Death's Shade

25th December, 2009

Harry Falconer spread garlic and tarragon butter evenly over the skin of the guinea fowl, wrapped it with fragrant whispers of Parma ham, and placed it lovingly in his cast-iron casserole dish, over a bed of sliced potatoes, julienne carrots, celery sticks, bay leaves and thinly sliced onion. This he placed in a wall cupboard, to keep it at room temperature and away from his Siamese's alter-ego, Mycroft, and his two more recently acquired cats, Tar Baby and Ruby, until it was time to pop it into the oven.

Returning to his sitting room, he surveyed with satisfaction the perfectly trimmed tree in the window, its fibre optics twinkling and reflecting in the copper and gold-coloured glass baubles that had complied with this year's colour co-ordinated design. Only gold lametta hung from its branches and, at its apex, he could almost hear the singing of the pure white plaster bird with its delicate touches of gold leaf, its tail and wings like gatherings of delicate glass threads; a bird of peace and glad tidings, rather like an avian angel.

No cards crowded his mantel; rather did they hang suspended on golden ribbons from the picture rail, even spaced around the room. The mantelpiece did, however, contain some gesture to the traditions of the season, in that it was draped in ivy, freshly bought the day before, and holly and mistletoe sat atop this where it topped the fireplace.

The radio was tuned to a Christmas morning Eucharist broadcast, and the blood-stirring harmonies of Tavener's 'The Lamb' floated through the air, dramatic, simple, yet complex at the same time, and inviting nostalgia and wonder anew at the Christmas story and its implications for mankind, but this latter meant little to Falconer. He was listening to this, as he had the Carols from King's, broadcast the day before.

His parents had never bothered about the religious aspects of Christmas, being too busy swilling champagne and cocktails, and entertaining, to let that sort of thing bother them. The real reason he turned on such broadcasts was because the army padre always insisted that, at Christmas, if at no other time in the church calendar, his 'lads' would get a bit of BBC church, whether they liked it or not (even if the men did sing alternative words to the carols, to bait their spiritual adviser, and draw his ire). Listening to these broadcasts, now that he had left the army, flooded Falconer with a warm glow of nostalgia.

Falconer's eyes swept over to the area below the tree, where a pile of small wrapped offerings had been meticulously arranged, and he smiled as he remembered what he had chosen for Mycroft, and the other two cats, and would present them with, after they had partaken of their meal. Then, of course, there would be the Queen's speech to attend to, something that had been part of his Christmas Day since as long as he could remember, and which he had never missed, no matter where in the world he had been.

He smiled contentedly, as he realised how right he had been to decline (impeccably politely) his family's invitations –

exhortations, even – to spend Christmas with them, their gaudy decorations, cocktail parties and false gaiety. For he had not grown to their pattern – he was not the social animal manqué; did not share their vast spider's web of friends, associates and acquaintances. Of course, their joint profession had fashioned their form, but he was different: he had not carried on the family tradition of the call of the Bar and had, as a result, become a more introspective person, who was happy both in his own skin, and company. He was self-sufficient, and at Christmas, as a rule, he was not a social animal.

As The Lamb gave way to a reading – And there were shepherds in the fields abiding – his contented reverie was shattered by the brash ringing of the telephone. He rolled his eyes, knowing it wasn't Aunt Ursula to wish him the compliments of the season, nor his mother Hermione with a last minute plea for him to join them and 'have some fun' for once in his life.

No, it would be work that was causing this untimely intrusion into the privacy of his celebrations, as it so often had in the past. Christmas was not a time of peace and goodwill, and of quiet contemplation, when you were a policeman. Picking up the telephone, he turned his steps back to the kitchen, to place his delectable but still raw game bird in the refrigerator.

It had been Superintendent 'Jelly' Chivers himself, who had summoned him, in tones both abrupt and imperious. Chivers never minced his words and, given the chance, called a spade a bloody shovel. He had risen to his present position through the ranks, with no buffer of a degree to set him on the road for fast-track promotion. It was said of him that, beneath his carapace of steel, lay a heart of pure flint. His diplomatic skills could be scored with a minus number, and it was rumoured in the staff canteen that he was an alien, originating from the planet 'Bastard'.

On the phone, Falconer was being told, and told good and proper. Chivers expected this whole mess to be cleared up today, and would accept no excuses for failure; failure, for him, being a dereliction of duty. As Falconer hung up, he thought, with a rueful smile, that old 'Jelly' would no doubt have a luxurious and happy day, celebrating in his own inimitable way, with his friends and family. What a pity the superintendent could not have left him alone, to celebrate Christmas in his own fashion.

Outside, the air was as sharp and biting as ice, a frost still underfoot. Overhead, thick banks of clouds were rolling in, to encase the day, as if under a Victorian glass dome – a December tableau to be picked up and shaken, to let loose the snowflakes for some giant child's amusement.

Pulling his cashmere scarf a little more securely over the shocked skin of his lower face, he headed towards his car, and the inevitability of what lay ahead of him. For one person at least, there was to be no Merry Christmas, no Happy New Year: just a pit of despair, loneliness, grief, and 'what ifs.' Life would go on, but not for one soul in the vicinity today, and for another it will be perceived as time standing still, as death mocks from the side-lines.

Shaking such sombre wraiths of thought from his mind, he started the engine of his car, and pondered on what he had learned from the telephone call. There had been a death in a block of apartments near the town centre. Not unusual at this time of year, for someone to depart this life, if only to avoid yet another Merry Christmas of jolly family arguments and seasonal acrimony, but it was usually an elderly or very sick person that chose this season of the year to shake off his or her mortal coil.

But this had been the death of a healthy young woman; in her prime, not at death's door. According to her fiancé, he had left her safe and well the previous evening, had let himself in with his own key this morning, for they had planned for him to move in with her on New Year's Day, only to find her dead, in the bed that was to have been theirs, in just a week's time.

There were no signs of a break-in, nothing was apparently missing, and there were no signs of violence on her body. It was her enjoyed youth and health that had flagged this as an unexplained death that would bear just the ghost of an investigation. A post mortem would probably provide a perfectly reasonable but unexpected cause but, for now, all avenues had to be explored, and this must be treated as it was being treated, as an unexplained death, with the police in attendance, in case there arose any hint of suspicion that this was an intended death, at the hands of another.

Superintendent Chivers had been more than forceful in his opinion of the rightness of their course of action, on today of all days. He had been insistent. He had a horror of unpleasantness in the press, and anti-police opinion, and was even prepared to interrupt the celebrations of the newly-appointed police surgeon to investigate the possibilities of a physical cause for her demise.

Acting DS 'Davey' Carmichael met him just outside the entrance lobby to the block of apartments, as unmoved by the slicing inclemency of the temperature as a giant would be by the passage of an ant. "Merry Christmas, sir," he boomed into the frozen void, his breath the phantom of a past bonfire, issuing from his lips in smoky clouds.

"Merry Christmas to you and yours, Carmichael," the inspector replied, and added, "and now we'd better get on with whatever awaits us here, for that'll be no merry Christmas. Why are such things sent at this time of year? Why does fate play games with the date for misfortune, ensuring there will be no other memories than this, on this day, every year, for the rest of people's lives?"

"Dunno, sir," mumbled Carmichael, almost looking upwards, as his superior's words shot over his head, to see if he could detect their flight-path. "Boyfriend's still up there, but the SOCO team's done its work, and they're just about to move the body. Better get up there, I suppose."

"You suppose right. It's really a public relations exercise for the old man, and his obsession with our relationship with the media, so the sooner we put our noses in, and declare everything clean and above board, the sooner we can get back to our respective households and recommence Christmas."

"Yes please, sir." Really, Carmichael was like a child – an exceedingly large child, notwithstanding – in his enthusiasm for this season of the year, and had been straining at the leash (more like a huge puppy now) since the first of December, eager for all the joys of Christmas shopping, Advent calendars, pine trees, paper streamers, cards, wrapping paper and carols. So intoxicated had the acting sergeant been by his seasonal love affair, that he had made Falconer seem like a re-incarnation of Ebenezer Scrooge himself.

Their office was hung with an abundance of paper chains and tinsel, a bunch of plastic mistletoe hung in the doorway, and a small silver tree stood on Carmichael's desk, hung with bright-coloured baubles, its lights winking on and off in an irritating way that drove Falconer nearly to distraction, and he couldn't wait for the New Year, so that his workspace could be returned to its normal, stark self.

This implied comparison to Scrooge, thought Falconer, wasn't really fair, as he had sent at least a dozen cards, bought gifts for the favoured few, decorated his home (according to his own lights – fibre-optic ones), and attended Midnight Mass the evening before. *So* he had no guests joining him today? *So* he was not spending the day with relatives or friends? Let Carmichael keep Christmas in *his* own way, and let him leave *him* alone, to celebrate it in *his.*

In the lobby of the building, they stopped to share what information they had gathered, from the phone calls that had separately summoned them to this address. Carmichael's call – lucky lad! – had originated from Bob Bryant, who was duty desk sergeant today. "Surely he's not on duty on Christmas Day? Does the man actually have no home to go to?" Falconer queried. The man was never off duty!

"He said the 999 call came through on the boyfriend's mobile. Apparently he just kept saying, "She's dead! She's dead! She's dead!" When Sergeant Bryant had managed to interrupt this three word obligato, he had been informed that the boyfriend and Miss Cater had spent the previous evening together, but he had returned to his own flat, so that he could wrap a very special present, which he planned to bring round this morning. He had already brought her other presents round to her apartment, but this had been something out of the ordinary, which she was not expecting."

"Lot of detail!" Falconer had commented.

"Seems that once Bob had got him going, he couldn't shut him up. 'Spose it must have been the shock. It gets some of them like that, doesn't it, sir? Anyway, he came round here, yesterday, late afternoon, they put up the tree – very last minute, because both of them had been so busy at work – then they had a meal and a quiet evening in. He left about midnight, he thinks, to go and wrap up this secret present, and not be too late to bed so that he could be round here first thing."

"Surely he could have wrapped her present at the office?"

Falconer's gaze moved slowly round the lobby in which they stood. The mansion block had been built in the thirties; outside, a tall, decorated pine tree stood to attention on each side of the double doors, each a fairy-land of white lights and silver stars. In here the lobby had been restored to its original character, obviously at some expense to the residents, and another large tree adorned this space: conveniently placed in a corner, beside the elevator doors. Its decorations were either original period pieces, or carefully copied reproductions.

The inspector's gaze, initially approving, shifted minimally to allow a shadow of uncertainty to enter his expression. One whole wall was taken up with burr walnut glass-fronted display cabinets, gleaming with the regular loving attention of beeswax. There were three of these, perfectly abutted, and all internally illuminated. The one on the left displayed a fine collection of Art Deco figurines in bronze, the one on the right, a similarly fine collection of elegant ladies, this time in impeccably painted porcelain.

It was the display cabinet in the middle that had given Falconer pause for thought. It boasted a proliferation of Clarice Cliff pieces, brazen in their gaudy rainbow hues and, although they were period-perfect to be included in this fine horde of objets d'art, he found their inclusion puzzling. The figurines, he could accept, but Clarice Cliff had originally been offered for sale in, of all places, Woolworth's.

In his opinion, the interior designer responsible for this ostentatious display of thirties finery, should have played the snob – so unacceptable in the twenty-first century – and realised, that, though the period was correct, the class was just *so* wrong. Becoming aware of Carmichael's voice, he shook his head to free his mind from such unworthy thoughts, and returned, reluctantly, to the here and now.

"What do we know about the deceased, Carmichael?"

"Twenty-three years old. Single. Angela Cater. Clerical officer for the local authority. No brothers or sisters, no pets, no children. Doesn't smoke, doesn't drink, doesn't take drugs."

"Golly, Bob must've got a right earful! Do we know if she rents, or owns the property?"

"Not yet, sir, but the bereaved gentleman will, no doubt, provide you with the information, if he's in the same loquacious state he was in when he phoned Bob."

"No doubt. Press the button for the lift. I'm beginning to suffer from era confusion, standing here."

STAVE TWO

The First Spirit – The Ghost of Christmas Ruined

The flat, when they entered it, was immaculately tidy, decorated, and dressed in the manner of its era. There was a proliferation of art deco furniture and knick-knacks, and the wallpaper and flooring were also in sympathy with this shift in time. Appropriate paper chains hung from the ceiling of the living room, which also housed a magnificent decorated fir tree, its presence made possible by the elegant proportions of the rooms of the apartment. At its foot were several brightly wrapped parcels, their wrapping paper blowing a raspberry to the art deco period and gaudily boasting their twenty-first century origins.

"Where was she found? In the bedroom? Which door do we need?" From their position just inside the front door they could see into the sitting room, but from the grand hall there were six other doors, all firmly closed to them.

At the sound of Falconer's voice, a door opened on the left-hand side of the hall, to reveal PC Green, Dr Christmas, and a white-faced young man, his head in his hands, seated at the stool in front of the dressing table. His position hid any view of the all too overwhelming presence of his girlfriend's body on the bed, eiderdown and bedclothes now flung aside, her nakedness barely concealed by a skimpy nightgown, incongruous in such dignified and respectable surroundings.

Seeing them at the door, Dr Christmas made to leave the room, leaving PC Green to guard the couple who had planned to spend the rest of their lives together, now irrevocably separated by the great black void of death.

"It's a bit of a stumper," commented Doc Christmas, scratching his head. "She was in perfect health before, but there are signs that she might have had some sort of severe allergic shock. Either that, or she's been poisoned. I won't have any firm idea, until I've sliced her open and done the business."

Falconer shuddered at the matter-of-fact way Christmas referred to the slicing and dicing of a post mortem, and hoped he'd never find himself under such off-hand hands (sic). "What I need to know is whether or not you suspect foul play?" stated the inspector.

"At this point, I've no idea. There was a Medic-Alert bracelet on the bedside table, indicating that she had an intolerance to peanuts, but the boyfriends said they were both vigilant, in ensuring that nothing that contained nuts ever entered the house.

"Apparently, if she travelled anywhere by plane, she would request that peanuts were not served to the other passengers, because of the re-circulated air – we really were better off when they stuck the smokers at the back of the plane, and pumped through fresh air, but that's an entirely different subject."

"I'll go and have a word with him myself," Falconer declared. "But, before I go in there, what's his name?"

"Dominic Cutler."

"Change the name and not the letter; change for worse, and not for better," piped up Carmichael, then subsided in a glowing blush, as the other two men shot him disapproving stares. "Sorry. I suppose it's the date they were going to move in together, that's unsettled me. That's the date that Kerry and I are going to get married."

"I know, Carmichael, I know. I'm going to be your best man, for my sins – may God have mercy on my soul – so I can hardly forget, can I?" said Falconer, with the look of a condemned man on his face.

"Oh, congratulations, Davey," added Dr Christmas, holding out a hand to shake the sergeant's.

"Thank you very much. I'm sorry about that comment just now. It just slipped out."

"Already forgotten, my boy. You've got work to do here, with old Harry, before you can kneel before the altar and plight your troth."

"I don't know what that means," said Carmichael, "referring to a church and all, but I hope it's not rude. And anyway, we're not having a big church 'do'. Remember Kerry's been married before, and she just wants something quiet and dignified."

"And a little less of the 'old', if you don't mind. You're a few years my senior, I know for a fact. Now, let's get back to the matter in hand," declared Falconer, firmly stamping on the tangent that had led them astray so effortlessly. "I need to speak to that chap in there, see what he has to say about last night, and that young lady's allergy."

He spoke to Dominic Cutler in the sitting room, just a few feet from the Christmas tree, and felt a heel for so doing, but he had little choice in the matter, not wanting to have to take the young man to the police station, on today of all days, for questioning.

"Tell me about yesterday, Mr Cutler; from the moment you left work, to the moment you arrived here this morning. I know how painful this must be for you, but we must get this matter cleared up. For all we know, someone with a key may have entered the premises during the night and murdered Miss Cater, so we need to know everything that we can about what happened in those hours. I'm sure you understand the necessity."

Dominic Cutler shook his head, as a dog does when getting out of water, maybe to clear his thoughts, so that he could converse in a rational manner.

"Let's start with where Miss Cater worked, and whether she owned this flat, or rented it," suggested Falconer, desperate to get the young man to tell him something – anything – to get him started.

"She worked for the local authority as a clerical officer, but she had no need to work: she did it because she needed something to occupy her time. Her parents are very wealthy – my God! This will destroy them – and actually own this apartment block, and this particular one's been signed over to her. That's why she lived here: so that she could have her independence, and still be under her father's care, if you see what I mean. If there had been any high jinks, it would have been reported to him by the concierge – complaints about noise, and that sort of thing."

"I completely understand, Mr Cutler. And what about you? Do you come from wealthy stock as well?" Falconer asked, hoping for an answer in the negative.

"As a matter of fact, I do," admitted Dominic. My parents have a huge house out in the countryside – quite isolated really – and it was them I went to see, after I'd wrapped Angela's tree presents yesterday, before I came here."

"Carry on," Falconer nudged him verbally, as he fell silent, and gazed off into the middle distance, maybe assessing the future life that would not now be his. Carmichael had tucked himself into a wooden-backed chair in a corner, folding himself on to its seat like a human ironing board, due to his height, and was busily taking notes, well-trained and needing no prompting, now that he was under Falconer's tutelage. Carmichael made a lot of furniture look as if it belonged in Lilliput, and not in people's everyday homes at all.

"We had originally planned to get married this Christmas, you see, but my father is very ill, and would not have been able to make the ceremony – that's why we postponed it, and I was just going to move in with her.

"I knew it would be the last Christmas Eve I would be able to do things the way that I had done them as a child. Father always used to read ghost stories, to everyone who was there for the celebrations, in front of a roaring fire, and crack nuts as he did so, for anyone who cared to have a munch on them. He wasn't fond of them himself, but he liked to crack them, and see others enjoying the 'nuts' of his labour. God! How can I make a pun when this has happened?" he asked, of no one in particular, except, maybe, himself.

"It was something my grandfather used to do," he continued, now recovered from the shock at his own unintentional words, "and he just carried on the tradition, as I had hoped to do, when Angela and I had a family to spend Christmas with." This last statement reduced the young man to tears again, and Falconer called in Dr Christmas, to see if he would give him a sedative, or something to make him sleep, then asked PC Green to run the bereaved man home, so that he could get some rest.

Unconscious was the best state for him, at the moment: a chance to let his mind work on all that had happened, and start to sort it out for him, so that he had everything in order, to deal with when he had had a little time for his subconscious to digest what had happened, and all the implications thereof. They could speak to him the next day, when maybe he'd be able to talk more coherently.

"Can you do something about opening her up?" Carmichael asked the doctor, a little stunned by the callous wording of his request.

"Nothing much on at the moment that can't wait," replied Christmas. "I can get on to it right away, if you want me to."

"Please. This peanut thing is nagging at me, and I need to know if she had any in her system that may have caused such a reaction. It would be a weird way to murder someone, giving them peanuts, disguised as something else, but nonetheless possibly effective. I just can't see a motive, though, can you, Carmichael?"

"What?" asked the big, friendly giant. "Oh, no, sir. Can't think of a thing." Carmichael had been gazing lovingly at the Christmas tree, with all the presents below it, no doubt imagining the fun and excitement going on in Jasmine Cottage, in Castle Farthing, where his fiancée Kerry lived, with her two sons from her previous marriage.

He could almost see them ripping off gay wrapping paper, and exclaiming in delight at what had been bought for them; almost smell the turkey, cooking slowly in the oven, and all the other trimmings as well; not forgetting the Christmas pudding. Kerry had made this one, and he was anxious to try it.

He had eaten there many times during their engagement, but this was their first Christmas together, and he hoped against hope, that her pudding was a suitable rival to his ma's, but maybe that was hoping for too much. Kerry was so perfect in every other way, in his opinion, that he could forgive her the Christmas pudding, if that proved necessary.

"Come on you, Davey Daydream! Let's get you back to the bosom of your family-to-be. There's nothing more here for us to do, today. But, I'd have thought you'd have been up to your eyes in wedding preparations, instead of having enough time to celebrate Christmas."

"No, that's all done and dusted, sir. Both families have been a real help in the arrangements, leaving me enough time to enjoy our first Christmas together."

"Oh, thank you very much, Carmichael. I never knew you cared," Falconer answered, smothering a smile. He had intentionally misinterpreted Carmichael's 'our first Christmas together', just to see how he reacted.

"Don't be silly, sir. Me, Kerry and the boys, I meant."

"I know you did. I was only pulling your leg. You get off and have a super day with them, and we'll carry on with this business, the day after tomorrow, if nothing urgent shows up. It's just bad luck, for everyone involved, that it's Christmas, but the day after Boxing Day's not quite so bad for being interrupted. Most people have had enough by then, and just want the whole business to be over and done with."

"You've no heart, sir. Where's your Christmas spirit?" asked Carmichael, bemused by the inspector's attitude to the season of goodwill.

"In my Christmas drinks' cupboard, where it belongs," answered Falconer, walking away from the day's unpleasant interruption, and thinking only of his own Christmas meal.

STAVE THREE

The Second Spirit – The Ghost of Christmas Restored

25th December, 2009 – a little later

When Carmichael returned to Castle Farthing where his fiancée lived (but where he would not reside until after their marriage, due to his old-fashioned moral principles), he found that Kerry had halted proceedings where they had left off, when he had so unexpectedly been called out.

The stocking presents had been opened, as they had been when he received the telephone call from Bob Bryant, but she had delayed the opening of the presents from under the Christmas tree, in the hope that Carmichael would not be gone all day, and she realised she had been right in her instincts, when he walked through the door, barely two hours after he had left.

"Daddy Davey!" the two boys, Kyle and Dean shouted, in their pleasure and excitement at his return. Not only was he back, to continue sharing Christmas Day with them, but now they could get at all the brightly wrapped packages and parcels nestling in a huge pile under the tree.

Ten minutes later, Carmichael was settled with his huge mug, filled with hot, very sweet tea (for he was no drinker), and the room was filled with the joyous shouts of children, ecstatic not only with what they had unwrapped, but with the sheer magical atmosphere of the day.

Back home, Falconer removed his guinea fowl from its temporary resting place, and popped it into the oven, which had only taken a few minutes to heat, and dealt with the rest of the trimmings that would accompany it for his, not quite solitary, Christmas meal, for he fully intended to share it with the cats, putting their bowls on the floor by the dining table, right next to his own place.

He hadn't quite worked out how he and Mycroft would pull a Christmas cracker together, nor how any of the cats would cope with being required to wear a paper hat, but these were mere details, and could wait until after they had finished eating, before he had to address them.

Finished in the kitchen, he removed the apron, which he had worn to protect his clothes, (he was very fastidious about his appearance), and removed three small parcels from under the tree, its fibre-optic lights with their ever-changing colours adding some seasonal cheer to the rather sparsely adorned room.

'Here you are, little friend," he said, calling Mycroft over to him. "This is for you, from me," and he proceeded to remove the wrapping paper for his pet. Inside was a small felt mouse, filled with 'cat-nip', which Mycroft immediately accepted delicately with his mouth, put down on to the floor, in order to give it a good sniff, then started to throw it up into the air and catch it, occasionally running across the room with it, to kill it to his complete satisfaction. Tar Baby and Ruby were just as pleased with their gifts, too.

There were several more little parcels in a similar vein, waiting for the already delighted animals, for the feline trio could smell the cooking, too, but Falconer would save those for later, when his pets tired of this first offering.

The smell of food floated enticingly on the air from the kitchen, making Falconer aware of its presence anew, and he sniffed, and sighed with anticipation at the gastronomic pleasures to come, in total agreement with his furry companions on this subject.

STAVE FOUR

A Seasonal Confection of Misdirection and Deceit

27th December, 2009 – morning

Carmichael called for Falconer in his old Skoda, seasonally trimmed with tinsel on its old-fashioned radio aerial and round the door handles, a tiny Christmas tree affixed to its parcel shelf.

"Did you have a nice Christmas, sir?" the sergeant asked, as soon as the inspector had taken his uncomfortable place in the clapped-out passenger seat, having had to brush aside empty crisp packets and chocolate bar wrappers so to do.

"I certainly had a nice peaceful time, and Mycroft, Tar Baby, Ruby and I listened to the Queen's speech together, as is our habit. What about you? How was your first Christmas with your family-to-be?"

"Absolutely fantastic, sir!" Carmichael declared, delight and happiness writ all over his face in large letters. "I can't believe my luck, when I remember what I was doing this time last year. I must be the luckiest man in the world, I reckon."

"I think that applies to all four of you, considering the circumstances under which you and Kerry met," replied Falconer, squirming and removing a now somewhat squashed tube of Smarties from underneath him. "We'll go to Cutler's apartment first, then on to his parents' house, then, finally on to Miss Cater's parents' place. PC Green and WPC Starr did the honours, with the distressing job of informing her parents of their daughter's death. Damned

31

charitable of them to volunteer. I must say, I didn't fancy doing it myself; not on Christmas Day, anyway."

"Me neither, sir. I think we owe them both a drink, to say thank you. Any news from Doc Christmas yet?" asked Carmichael, receiving an answer in the negative, which wasn't surprising really, considering the time of year. He'd no doubt be in touch, as soon as he had anything for them.

Dominic Cutler's address turned out to be in an apartment block, of a similar housing class to that of his late fiancée, and he answered their ring at the external intercom with surprising promptness, almost as if he had been waiting for them, which, of course, he had. He had hardly slept since Christmas Day morning, despite being given something to aid him in that respect, and was desperate to know what they had discovered about Angela's death.

Inside, the flat was luxuriously appointed, but without overwhelming the visitor with its occupier's obvious wealth. Everything was discreet, the colours muted, the atmosphere airy and relaxing. Dominic begged them to be seated and make themselves comfortable – his manners impeccable now the first shock had worn off.

"I wonder if you can tell me about your movements, in detail, from when you went to your parents' house on Christmas Eve, to when you found Miss Cater's body on Christmas morning?" asked Falconer. Carmichael was seated slightly out of sight-line, so that his note-taking should remain discreet, and not unnerve the bereaved young man.

"I know we went over this on Christmas Day, but I'd just like to recap, in case you've remembered something you forgot to tell me before, in your distress."

"No problem!" answered Cutler. "I just called round to see them, knowing it would be the last Christmas my father saw. He's suffering from cancer, and is in the latter stages now. It won't be long, for him, now – Last Chance Saloon, as it were. As I told you on Christmas Day, we just did the ordinary traditional things that we always did on Christmas Eve: the telling of ghost stories, and the cracking of nuts.

"My mother gave me a rather valuable necklace for Angela, as a Christmas present. It was one of the pieces of family jewellery, that she wanted her to have, now that she was going to be a member of our family. I concealed it in my wallet, when I went round to Angela's, because I wanted to go home and wrap it, as a surprise for Christmas Day.

"When I got to her flat, everything was just as normal, or as normal as it can be at this time of year. We were to spend the next day together, and she was already fussing about the ingredients for the Christmas meal. You know how women are!

"She put a CD of carols on while she buzzed about in the kitchen, and I looked on, not daring to try to get involved, in case I made her lose concentration. Then we went into the living room, and she put on a DVD of Dickens' *Christmas Carol* – the one with Alec Guinness. 1954, I think it was made, but it's the absolute best one, and we put up the tree, which was a bit of a monster, but suited her place perfectly well.

"After that, we ... we ... er ... went to bed for a while." Revealing such an intimate detail had obviously embarrassed Dominic, and his narrative ground to a halt.

"Thank you very much for being so frank with us, Mr Cutler. Dr Christmas said there was evidence of sexual activity, and you have just given us a rational explanation for that. Please carry on," Falconer encouraged him.

"Then I came back here, wrapped the necklace for the next day, and went to bed. There's nothing else to tell, except for me going round to Angela's apartment, the next morning, letting myself in, a little bit pleased that she had not yet woken, so that I could play Father Christmas with the necklace from my mother. I knew she'd love it, and would probably wear it on our wedding day."

"Do you have a date for that, Mr Cutler?"

"No, we hadn't got round to that yet. We wanted it to be Christmas Eve, but, with my father being so ill, we decided that I'd move in here on January the first, and we'd set a date ... afterwards – you know. When my father had ... gone."

"You have a lot to cope with, emotionally, at the moment, but I must press you to tell us of your discovery of Miss Cater's body," said Falconer, feeling like a louse. The young man had postponed his wedding, and lost his fiancée, and all the while, his father was dying a slow and painful death. Life could be a fair cow at times, he thought.

"I went into the flat, and stopped and listened. There was only silence, which I thought confirmed my first idea, that she was still asleep in bed, and that mine would be the first face she saw on Christmas Day, and I put my hand into my overcoat pocket, just to check that I hadn't forgotten the necklace in my hurry to get over there.

"I went into the bedroom, and she had her back to me, the covers all over the place, as usual. She was a very restless sleeper. That made me smile; how I would surprise her by waking her ..." Again his voice trailed off, and he put his head in his hands. "I'm sorry, but this is really difficult," he mumbled, rubbing at his eyes, as if there were grit in them.

"I crept over to the bed, and put my hand on her shoulder, but it was unnaturally cold. That made me feel a bit anxious, so I gave a little pull at her, to make her turn over, and then I saw ..."

"That's all right, Mr Cutler. We know what you saw. And you're perfectly sure that there weren't any peanuts in her apartment, in any shape or form, when you left it on Christmas Eve?"

"I'm positive. Angela was paranoid about the things. Shopping with her was a nightmare. She had to read every label, to see what was in everything, and if it even said 'may contain traces of nuts' she avoided the product, even if it hadn't specified 'peanuts', saying that she couldn't be too careful, given the severity of her allergy.

"She was due to have more hospital tests in the New Year, to ascertain whether her allergy also included other nuts, so she was extra vigilant in everything she bought, and we never ate out, just in case. In fact, we hardly went anywhere. She couldn't go to pubs or bars because of other people eating peanuts, and she couldn't trust the recipes in restaurants. In fact, the only places we've ever been together are the cinema and the theatre.

"I think that's all we need to know, for now, except, do you know if anyone else had a key to Miss Cater's apartment?"

"Except for me, only her parents, in case of emergency," he answered, looking a little calmer.

"And how long had you known Miss Cater?"

"Only about three months. It was love at first sight, followed by a whirlwind romance – all those terrible clichés were true, for us."

"Oh, and would it be possible to speak to your parents, just to confirm the events on Christmas Eve?" Falconer slipped in at the last minute.

"I'd rather you didn't go to the house. My father's in a bad way at the moment: in a lot of pain, and heavily sedated, but if you'd like to call back here tomorrow, about five o'clock, my mother is going to come over to see me, to discuss … arrangements. She doesn't like to do that where Daddy or the nurse might possibly overhear – not even on the telephone – so she'll be visiting me in the afternoon, and I can give her back the necklace, at the same time. There's no use me hanging on to it, now that Angela's dead," Dominic explained.

"That seems perfectly acceptable," replied Falconer. "We just need corroboration of your story, for our records. I wonder if you'd let us have a look at the necklace, before we go."

"Of course. Here it is," Cutler replied, pulling it out of a small drawer in a desk just behind him.

It was a real beauty! Light sparked from it, in myriad rainbows of colour, which reflected on the walls and ceiling, and made moving patterns of light as Falconer turned it this way and that. "Thank you very much, sir," he commented, handing it back. "It's a lovely old piece. I'm sure Miss Cater would have loved and cherished it."

"So am I," replied Cater, in a faltering voice. "I'll just show you out."

STAVE FIVE

A Christmas Gift of Pertinent Information

27th December, 2009 – afternoon

As they now had no need to visit Dominic Cutler's parents, Falconer and Carmichael shared a companionable lunch in 'The Shoulder of Mutton and Gherkins'. This was the first suspicious death that they had worked on that had actually taken place in Market Darley, and, for once, they had no need to dash about the countryside to some far-flung village. It all seemed terribly civilised.

"I'm sorry I haven't had the opportunity to ask you yet, but are you having a nice Christmas, Carmichael?" Falconer asked his sergeant, and was suddenly flooded with a perfect cataract of a narrative, about this 'first of many' Christmas and Boxing Days.

"They'd waited for me, when I got back on Christmas morning. The boys hadn't opened any of the presents from under the tree. They'd put it off until I got back, so that I could share in their excitement. Wasn't that thoughtful of them all?

"And Kerry's Christmas dinner was easily as good as anything my ma's ever cooked. We listened to the Queen, then the boys played with all their new toys. Oh, and the Christmas pud! It was the most delicious I've ever tasted – absolutely first rate, and made to one of Kerry's godmother's family recipes. You remember Alan and Marian

Warren-Browne from the post office in Castle Farthing,
don't you?" he asked.

Falconer was given only enough time to agree that he did,
indeed, remember them, before the momentum of
Carmichael's narrative resumed. "We had a cracking tea,
with fruit, jelly and ice-cream, Christmas cake, and mince
pies and sausage rolls. It was all top-notch scoff." Carmichael
needed to consume a lot, to fuel a frame as large as his, so his
mind was frequently preoccupied with food – what he had
already eaten, and when and what he would eat in the future,
given the opportunity.

"The next day we did something that is a tradition in my
family, and Kerry had never heard of before. My ma realised,
a long time ago, how children ache for just one more present,
on Boxing Day, after all the excitement of the day before, so
she always used to wrap a little something for everyone, and
hang the parcels from the Christmas tree. Then, when we
came down on Boxing Day, after breakfast, we used to get to
open what she referred to as 'the tree presents', and it was just
a lovely little extra, to all the presents from the day before.

"Anyway, we did this after breakfast on Boxing Day, and the
boys loved it. Then, after lunch – oh, the lunch! Tons of
cold meats, oodles of pickles, and the most buttery mashed
potatoes you could imagine, sir. Kerry and the boys had a
load of salad stuff, as well, but I couldn't be bothered with
that – there was too much other lovely stuff to get through.

"Anyway, after that lot, I went up to get what I had hidden
in Kerry's wardrobe, when I originally arrived, and came
downstairs with a little sack of presents, with numbers stuck

on them – it's another tradition in the Carmichael family, that there is a 'lucky dip', and I'd kept this as a surprise.

"Everyone pulls a number out of a hat (ready and waiting, of course), and chooses the present with the matching number. There should be loads of little gifts: tiny, inexpensive things, like a comb or a lollipop, so that it doesn't get too costly. It can, in fact it did, last all the afternoon.

"We had an absolutely smashing time. What about you, sir?"

The tirade suddenly stopped. The whirlwind ceased, and left Carmichael staring in enquiry at the inspector.

"Very nice, thank you, Carmichael," Falconer replied.

Mr and Mrs Cater lived in a very large detached house, about a mile outside Market Darley, with about five acres of garden – or grounds. Falconer couldn't decide exactly how he would describe the land they had.

The door was opened by a housekeeper, who bade them enter, and showed them into the morning room, where they awaited the bereaved parents. Alan and Edith Cater joined them, a few minutes later, grief still marking their faces, their footsteps slow, as if nothing were of any importance any more.

After the usual introductions, and expressions of sympathy for their loss, Falconer apologised for bothering them, and said he would keep their visit as short as possible, so that they could be left in peace, to come to terms with what had happened.

"I'd like to ask you how well you knew your daughter's fiancé. Did he come here a lot? Did you ever go to his home, or meet his parents?" Falconer began his questioning, as Carmichael, inevitably, prepared to do his version of shorthand.

"He came here once, very briefly, just so that we could meet him, but they had to rush off somewhere – I can't remember where, now – the theatre, or a cinema, or some such place. He seemed a nice enough young man, but we were a little concerned, at the speed at which their relationship was developing," Alan Cater informed them.

"Why was that?"

"Because of the amount of money that Angela would in– would have inherited, should anything happen to us. We didn't want her to get involved with a gold-digger. But he seemed a nice enough young man. We went to his apartment, once, for a drink before a function we were attending in Market Darley, and he seemed to be very comfortably off, so it set our minds at rest," Edith Cater continued, on her husband's behalf.

"I suppose, with the tests she had booked for the New Year, they would have discovered something else she was allergic to, if she died of an allergic reaction." Mrs Cater couldn't go on, and her husband took over.

"I presume that Cutler knew all about the peanut thing, and didn't just make a mistake, did he?"

"He certainly explained her condition to us, in some detail, and said that he always avoided peanuts, or anything that had them in it, for her sake," Falconer informed them.

"Well, I suppose the proof of that will be in what the post mortem discovers, won't it?" Mr Cater asked, his face a white mask of disbelief and disgust. "Children aren't supposed to die before their parents. It's an obscenity, if you think about it. No one should ever be asked to bury their child," he added, visibly trying to pull himself together.

"We'll leave you in peace now," Falconer said, having decided that they'd got the information they'd come for, and would burden the bereaved parents no longer with their company.

Back at the office, Dr Christmas rang Falconer, with some preliminary findings from the post mortem. "It was definitely a severe allergic reaction that killed her, Harry, but I can't seem to determine what triggered it. I've been through the stomach contents with a fine-tooth comb – if you'll pardon the ghastly phrasing – and I can't find any trace of peanuts. In fact, I can't find traces of any other sort of nut, either, in there. Her stomach was definitely a nut-free organ, and I don't know what to make of that.

"I'm going to have a look through some learned journals now, and then look on the internet, and consult a couple of colleagues, to see if I can come up with anything, but, frankly, I hardly know what to look for, let alone ask about," he concluded, his voice sounding as puzzled as he felt.

"The reaction must have been triggered by something, and I expect you to work your clinical little socks off, to find out what it was. We must know the reason for that reaction having been triggered. Anything less will leave the lot of us looking like a bunch of rank amateurs," was Falconer's reply.

"I'll carry on for now, and give you a ring in the morning. I hope I'll know more by then. Bye for now." And the doctor was gone, no doubt, back to his own detective work, to explain the demise of his current 'customer'.

STAVE SIX

The Third of the Spirits – The Spirit of Justice

28th December, 2009 – morning

About ten o'clock on the morning of the twenty-eighth, Falconer received another phone call from Dr Christmas, this time with some very interesting information, which he promised to e-mail to CID, so that it could be recorded in the official file, and which confirmed that Angela Cater did have a nut allergy that was more far-ranging than just peanuts. One final quirky fact made up Falconer's mind for him.

Doc Christmas had located the site of the allergen, and declared he had never come across anything like it in his whole professional life, before. The inspector would be going to see that young man again, this afternoon, but he'd go prepared for what he intended to do, and he'd face Cutler with what he'd just been told.

Carmichael's mouth dropped open in disbelief, when Falconer related the contents of the call from Dr Christmas to him, and it took some while for him to believe that Falconer wasn't just pulling his leg, to see how gullible he was.

"I promise you, Carmichael, that's the God's honest truth. I've checked it out myself, for much the same reason as you suspected me of: of having you on, but it's true. I'd never have guessed it was possible, but apparently it is, and we've just got to accept it, and what it implies."

"But she hadn't eaten any nuts?"

"None whatsoever, Carmichael. Her stomach was as clean as the proverbial whistle of traces of any nuts of any sort."

"I've done a couple of other checks on various things that we've been told, and I think I'm as prepared as I can be for this afternoon's visit."

28th December, 2009 – afternoon

When they reached the apartment block that Cutler had given as his address, Falconer noticed for the first time that the name in the little holder by the intercom was written on a tatty piece of paper, by hand, and not printed on card, like the others above and below it.

Why had he not noticed that before? Probably because he couldn't have imagined the bizarre turn that events were about to take, and had accepted everything at face value – a very dangerous and unprofessional thing for a detective to do.

A resident on the way out passed the open door to them so there was no need to ring the doorbell. This was just as well, as it would give their arrival the element of surprise that having to ring would not have done.

The door was opened, with only a wait of thirty seconds or so, during which, voices could be heard from within, and then Mr Cutler was there, in the doorway, inviting them inside, to meet his mother. There was definitely a familial resemblance between him and the woman who rose from a sofa to greet them, but, with the information he now possessed, Falconer was able to discern easily that there was something not quite right about the way she was dressed.

"Your arrival has just reminded me that I promised to return that necklace to my mother today," commented Cutler, moving to the desk, whence he had extracted it previously to show to Falconer.

"I'd be grateful if you'd pass that to me, if you don't mind, sir," Falconer requested, noting a little frown of anxiety cross Cutler's face.

"Of course. No problem. Is there something wrong, Inspector?"

"There most definitely is, Mr Cutler, but fortunately I've been able to put the pieces of the jigsaw puzzle together, and see the whole picture, and not just the part of it that you wanted me to see."

"What are you talking about? I don't understand what's going on here."

"Oh, I think you do, sir, as does your mother. I am arresting you for the wilful murder of Angela Rebecca Cater on 24th December, 2009 ..." the official caution followed, then Falconer turned his attention to Mrs Cutler.

"Mrs Rita Lesley Cutler, I am arresting you, for withholding of evidence, in a case of murder – oh, and probably some other things as well, when I can get round to working out what they are. You don't live in some big house in the country with a dying husband, do you? You live in a council house on the Wild Birds Estate, on the outskirts of Market

Darley, and your husband did a runner, years ago. I've got a patrol car, which should now be waiting outside for us, so I'm asking you to come quietly, or I'll have to call the occupants of said patrol car up here, to help you to cooperate."

"I told her I'd love her to death, Inspector," Cutler shouted, as he was escorted out of the flat. "After a while, she used to beg me, when we were having sex 'Oh, love me to death, Dom. Love me to death,' she'd moan, so on Christmas Eve, I did."

"Come on, sir, give! There're lots of pieces to this particular jigsaw puzzle that I don't know about, so spill the beans, or I'll have to get PC Green to frighten the truth out of you."

They were back in the office now, and Carmichael, who had not been party to much of the digging that Falconer had done, was waiting with baited breath to hear the whole story.

"Apparently it had all started when Dominic, in his usual guise of an habitual layabout, in scruffy clothes and with wild, unkempt hair, had gone into the council offices to report a blocked drain. He was living at home with his mother, both of them on benefits, in one of the local authority houses out in 'the wilds' of the Wild Birds Estate, and on that particular visit to the local authority, it was Angela who took the details from him.

"I don't know how he found out things about her, but he obviously did, and became obsessed with her, as well as her wealth, and he thought he could do himself a bit of good, if he got to know her. Anyway, he spruced himself up a bit and got a decent haircut, then he had a stroke of luck that he could not have foreseen.

"An old school-friend of his, who had prospered, was going away, on a six-month contract, to Dubai. They had always been particular friends at school. This friend knew how Dominic was fixed, still living at home with his mother, and, very generously in my opinion, asked him if he'd like to move into his apartment while he was away, to keep an eye on it, otherwise it would be standing empty – a magnet for anyone with evil intentions, who could manage to get inside it.

"Of course, Cutler jumped at the chance. Now, he could engineer a meeting with Angela Cater, and not only look the part, but have the right address, to go with the manufactured background he was going to feed to her.

"He was the one who really made the running in the relationship, Angela just getting carried away with the romance, probably, and swept off her feet, with the speed with which things happened. He never let her visit his family, because the family he'd told her about simply didn't exist. But he did get her to make a will, in his favour, when they'd talked about marriage, explaining that it was best to do it straight away, even if their marriage nullified it, as anything could happen to anyone, in the blink of an eye, and he would do the same for her.

"He took a bit of a risk with his plan to kill her, but it obviously paid off, as we all found out only three days ago. His friend had left behind a diamond necklace that belonged to his grandmother, and had asked Cutler to get it cleaned, before leaving for Dubai – this was a vital piece of evidence, should his plan come off. If it didn't, he just wouldn't mention it, and would have returned it to his friend on his return to this country. It was really the only thing he had with which to fool us about his wealth, but it was a risk he was willing to take.

"He knew that any nuts found in Angela's stomach at the post mortem, might point the finger directly at him, so he couldn't risk that happening. But he did stumble across a little known fact about Brazil nuts that suited his purposes perfectly."

"And that was what Dr Christmas rang up and told you about?" asked Carmichael, sitting with his chin resting in his hands, as attentive as a child being read a particularly enjoyable story.

"That's right, Carmichael. Cutler had found out that eating Brazil nuts would cause traces of them to be passed on through sexual contact"

"So his nuts contained traces of nuts?" asked Carmichael, with a wide grin at his witticism.

"Don't be coarse, Sergeant!" replied Falconer, and then dissolved into mirthful laughter, not just at the witticism, but at Carmichael's crestfallen face at this rebuke. "Anyway, to continue, he then stuffed himself with them all day on Christmas Eve, hoping that he'd eaten enough, and given them enough time to get through his system. Then, as we know, he made love to Miss Cater, just before he left her apartment on Christmas Eve."

"Bastard!" commented Carmichael casually, hoping not to interrupt the inspector's flow.

He didn't, as Falconer continued, "She was probably already showing signs of her allergic reaction before he left, but he stayed on to make sure that she was in no condition to phone for help, or leave the apartment, to seek it elsewhere.

"The next day, he knew exactly what he would find, when he turned up at her door, and, I must say, in my opinion he turned out to be a pretty good actor."

"But how did you suss out all that other stuff, sir?" Carmichael asked, with a face that indicated that he regarded all the other facts garnered as nothing short of magic.

"Simple, and all of it readily available to be found. I thought it was a bit iffy, that Cutler had never taken her to his family home to meet his parents, and then he didn't want me to visit them either. Was that because they didn't exist, or because there was something very wrong about his background?

"I contacted the concierge of the block that he's been living in, confirmed that the apartment had been sub-let to him, with the permission of the lease-holder, and got said lease-holder's contact number, should anyone need to be contacted in an emergency. I also got a contact number for the real tenant, in Dubai.

"A quick phone call to Dubai confirmed that Dominic Cutler was no more the affluent young man about town than Bob Bryant is, and that he was only living there, to give him a break from living with his mother in a council house, to try to sort himself out, find himself a job, and gain a little more self-respect.

"Well, he'd done more than that. He'd found himself a wealthy young woman. All he had to do was, literally, love her to death, as he told us so callously."

"God, that's evil, sir," Carmichael commented, sitting up straight, as he realised that Falconer had reached the 'and they lived unhappily ever after' point of his story.

"He'll get his comeuppance, and he won't get a penny from that will, either," stated Falconer. It might just have worked, however, with less diligent officers, too bound up in their own families, at this particular time of year, to do much digging.

"He was prepared for us to come round and give him the tragic news, that Brazil nuts are something that can be transmitted from one body to another during sexual intercourse, and would have played the broken-hearted fiancé who had lost his beloved, because he had accidentally and unknowingly killed her, by making love to her – loved her to death, in fact.

"How that phrase makes me shudder, when I think about it! Instead, he got the spirit of justice, rather than the spirit of Christmas, and the next season of goodwill he sees will be from the inside of a prison cell. And that's just how it should be.

"What an audacious plan, and to think that he thought he could fool the police like that! Well, I suppose we'd better be getting off home."

"Would you like to come to ours for your tea, sir? Kerry's promised that she's got the most delicious recipe in the world, for cold curried turkey, and there are loads of mince pies, and a whole hunk of Christmas ham left."

"I don't know, Carmichael. I'd planned on a quiet night in."

"On your own again, I suppose," declared the sergeant, with both disapproval, and concern.

"With my pets, Carmichael."

"Well, I won't hear of it! Those cats can stay on their own, for one evening. You're coming home with me, and having some proper seasonal company, for a change, you miserable old Scrooge, and I'll not take 'no' for an answer," the sergeant stated with vehemence.

"That's very hospitable of you, Carmichael, but are you sure Kerry won't mind?"

"Mind? She'll be over the moon! She's been dying for you to visit: she's heard so much about you."

"From you, Carmichael?" asked Falconer, apprehensively.

"Of course from me, sir."

"Oh, dear!" said Falconer, following, Carmichael out of the room, to his uncertain fate, that evening.

STAVE SEVEN

The Fourth Spirit – The Spirit of Christmas Yet to Come

28th December, 2009 – evening

Falconer was surprised and secretly delighted to be welcomed, as an honoured guest, at the cottage in Castle Farthing where Carmichael would live after his marriage, in just a few days' time. Kerry was obviously delighted to welcome such an important figure into her home, and the two boys, who treated Carmichael's position as a detective sergeant with casual contempt, were thrilled to have a real detective inspector visit their home.

The cottage was decorated in a suitably over-the-top festive manner, and some work had been done to connect the rooms with the cottage next door. A much too tall fir tree dominated the front room, drowning under its own weight of baubles, tinsel, and other seasonal ornamentation. In the grate, a wood fire was burning, and the whole atmosphere was redolent of the sort of Christmas that Falconer had never experience before, and it filled him with an unexpected joy.

Carmichael was a very luck young man, to be moving into this home, with its convivial and welcoming occupants, devoid of any of the airs and graces that would have been present at one of his parents' Christmases.

Flopping down into an armchair by the fire, indicated to him by Kerry, he accepted the half pint of beer that Carmichael thrust into his hand, and prepared to enjoy himself, with not even a hint of the 'keeping up appearances' attitude that had , and probably still did, prevail in his family home, for the first time in years.

The End of it

"Why don't you come for Christmas Day, next year, sir?" asked Carmichael, seeing Falconer relaxed and perfectly at ease at the fireside.

"I might just take you up on that offer, Carmichael," Falconer mumbled, feeling his eyes droop, in the warm and welcoming atmosphere of the little home. "I might just do that!"

Maybe Christmas wasn't so bad after all!

THE END. . . . . until the next time!

A Sidecar Named Expire

A young man and his girlfriend decide to celebrate their first St Valentine's Day together, with a cosy evening of cocktails at her house. But as the evening progresses, events don't go quite as Malcolm Standing planned.

The next morning, DI Falconer and DS Carmichael are called in to try to sort out what really happened.

Chapter One

14th February

'Now, my cocktail starts with one-and-a-half measures of gin.'
There was a short glugging sound from round the angle of the L-shaped
room, as Chelsea Fairfield began to mix the drinks with which they
were going to celebrate their first St Valentine's Day together.

They had only been an item for three weeks or so, but Malcolm
Standing had been captivated by her since their first meeting, and
had gladly accepted her invitation to spend this evening at her house,
drinking cocktails together. He had high hopes of not going home at all
tonight, and sprawled on the sofa in an ecstasy of expectation. Tonight
would probably be the night!

'One-and-a-half measures of Cointreau,' her voice purred on, 'and
one-and-a-half measures of lemon juice. Shake,' he discerned the quiet
sloshing of the cocktail shaker being agitated, 'and strain into a frosted
glass, over ice. There! That's my White Lady sorted. Now for your
Sidecar.'

'How come I don't get to choose my own cocktail?' he called out to
her.

'You can after the first one. I just thought a Sidecar was rather
appropriate, as you ride a motorbike,' she called in answer, and
Malcolm could feel his whole body tingling in anticipation of the
evening to come.

'Right! A Sidecar. Bit of information for you here, my dear. This
cocktail was originally created after the First World War, in 'Harry's
Bar' – the one in Paris, not the one in Venice, and was named after an
officer who used to go there by chauffeur-ridden motorcycle sidecar.
See what I mean?

'And now for the ingredients. One measure of cognac, one measure
of Cointreau, and one measure of lemon juice.' As she shook the
cocktail, he raised his voice to give his opinion of the two recipes.

'Yours seems to be half as strong again as mine. Why's that? It doesn't seem fair to me.'

'Just think about it, sweetie,' she answered, and he heard her speaking in a slightly quieter voice. 'There we go! And strain, garnish with a slice of lemon, over crushed ice. I'm on my way.'

In less than a minute, she came round the 'L', carrying a small silver tray with the two glasses on it.

'Hand it over, then,' Malcolm said, holding out his hand.

'Not just yet, big boy. I want the occasion to be just right, so, just before we drink our cocktails, I want us to enjoy a black Russian cigarette.'

'But I don't smoke!' he protested.

'Neither do I,' she replied, 'but trust me, this is definitely the best way to enjoy these cocktails,' and in so saying, she removed a small black box from a drawer in a wall unit, opened it, and held it out for him to take a cigarette, took one herself, and produced a lighter to light them. 'Now,' she ordered, 'a couple of puffs on that, and we can have our glasses. Happy Valentine's Day, darling.'

'And the same to you ... darling.' He hesitated over the last word, as this was the first time that they had used it, but he got over his surprise by gazing at the huge bouquet of flowers that he had brought with him, and thought that they had been worth the money, if this was the effect they had on her.

While all this was going through his mind, he was having difficulty not to succumb to a fit of coughing from the cigarette smoke. He had tried smoking when he was about nine or ten, but it had made him throw up, and he just hoped that this unfortunate consequence did not recur this evening. How that would ruin things for him!

Asking for an ashtray, he took a token puff on the cigarette and put it down in the corner of the receptacle, looking pleadingly towards the two glasses on the tray.

'You can have your drink, now,' Chelsea purred, and placed the tray under his nose with a flourish. 'Enjoy!' she said, taking her own glass, and setting the tray down on the wall unit where it had sat in the meantime.

Only a few minutes later, Chelsea stood up and announced that she was going to mix them another drink. 'What, already?' he asked.

'Yes! Come along, slow coach. Get that down your neck, and we can have another one before seeing how events develop.' Eager at the promise in her words, he downed the last of the liquid in the cocktail glass and watched as she disappeared behind the 'L' again.

'That seemed awfully strong,' he said, raising his voice a little so that she could hear him, and realised that his head was beginning to spin.

'I'll cut down on the measures this time, if it's a problem for you,' she called back. 'And don't forget to have a couple of puffs on your cigarette. They're dead expensive, they are, and if I don't see you smoking it when I get back round there, I'm going to be very cross with you.'

'But I don't like 'em,' he replied, realising that his voice was beginning to slur.

'I don't care! I'm educating you in the finer things in life, and you'll do as I say, or else!'

When she came back to him this time, she put down the tray, extracted two more cigarettes from the box, and lit them both, handing one to him, but when he reached for it reluctantly, he seemed to have two hands on the end of his arm. 'Blimey!' he thought. 'The things that blokes do, just to get a leg-over.'

Putting the slightly smoked cigarette down in the ashtray, he held his hand out for his glass containing his second Sidecar of the night.

As he supped the cold liquid, he took a moment to protest. 'I thought you 'ere goin' to le' me cock my own choose-tail, af'er the firs' one,' he complained, listening to the deterioration in his speech with puzzlement.

'You can choose the next one, my darling,' she soothed him, holding up her glass in salutation to encourage him to drink more of his.

Malcolm had no idea of the time, but it seemed to be a lot later, and he was incapable of moving, and barely capable of thinking. Chelsea was telling him something, but he couldn't understand what she was saying. It seemed to be in a foreign language; one that he had never heard before.

He was aware of her tucking his feet up on the sofa, and removing his shoes and the cocktail glass, which his right hand had still been clutching. How many had he had? He had no idea. His memory was a blank. Slowly his eyelids closed over his reluctant eyes, and he slept.

Chapter Two

15th February

The voice on the phone was breathless with urgency. 'But he's dead, and he's on my sofa, and I don't know what to do about it. Please send someone as quick as you can. It's so horrible, looking at him just lolling there and ... well, being dead, I suppose.

'I've given you the address, but I can't bear to sit here looking at him any longer, so I'm going round to my next door neighbour's. I'll watch for the car from there. Please be quick. This is doing my head in. Oh, I know that sounds awful, but it's just not *him* anymore, it's an 'it', and it's really giving me the willies.

'God knows what happened. He must have had a weak heart, or something. All I know, as I told you, is that he's dead, and in my house, and I simply can't cope with that a moment longer than I have to. Goodbye.'

Desk Sergeant Bob Bryant put down the telephone receiver and made a quick decision to alert Detective Inspector Harry Falconer and his partner, Detective Sergeant Davey Carmichael. This one sounded right up their street, and shouldn't take too long to wrap up once Dr Christmas had got the poor gentleman on the table and opened him up.

Using the internal phone service, he rang through to Falconer to send him and his sergeant on their way, then went back to an external line to contact Dr Philip Christmas to attend the scene as well. As it was an unexpected death, he decided to send a small SOCO team as well. It was better to be safe than sorry, he'd always found, and if things didn't turn out as simply, as he was almost sure they would, it would be in his favour if he had dotted all the i's and crossed all the t's.

Following that flurry of activity, he called one of the uniformed PCs, who had just wandered in, to take over at the desk for ten minutes while he went for a cup of coffee. It was thirsty work, holding the fort at

Market Darley Police Station, and he needed a break after that sudden burst of activity.

'It's not far, so we'll take my car,' DI Falconer decided as he and DS Carmichael exited the station, noticing that Bob Bryant was no longer on the desk. 'What was that address again, Carmichael?'

'Twelve Coronation Terrace – built just after the coronation of our present Queen,' he observed, displaying, as usual, more local knowledge than Falconer would have believed could exist in the young man's head. He had recently got married, and seemed, if possible, even happier than he had been when he was first partnered with Falconer the previous summer.

In fact, it was during the previous summer, on their first case together, that Carmichael had met the young woman who had recently become his wife, and he lived with her and her two sons from a previous marriage in the village of Castle Farthing, the locus for said first case.

It only took ten minutes to reach Coronation Terrace, and as they slowed to read the numbers of the houses, a woman came out of one of them stepped over the low dividing front garden wall to the house next door and beckoned to them to stop.

'I've got 'er in 'ere,' she informed them, indicating her own house by the bending of her head in the direction of her front door. 'She's in a terrible state, poor little thing. Such a dreadful thing to 'appen, when you're as young as she is. She can 'ardly take it in, nor neither can I. I'm Ida Jenkins – Mrs – by the way.'

The woman was in her late sixties, and had a motherly look about her. A comfortably round figure with an apron tied over the front of it was presented between sensible carpet slippers and wrinkled stockings at the bottom, and a mop of greying curls and a sympathetic face at the top. She looked kind; just the sort of neighbour one would want to have in an emergency.

'You come on in,' she exhorted them, stepping back over the wall on to her own path. 'She's inside, with a small glass of brandy to perk 'er up. You go in an' see 'er, and I'll make us all a nice cup of tea. I reckon I've got an unopened packet of chocolate digestives in my kitchen cupboard as well. Nothin' like tea to raise the spirits, my old ma used to say, and she was right, too.'

She led them into her living room, which had not been knocked through in the way that many of the houses had, and they found a young woman sitting on the only sofa, quietly crying into a handful of tissues. 'Chelsea Fairfield?' enquired Falconer.

At the sound of his voice she looked up, displaying red eyes and a face made puffy by weeping. Unable to manage a spoken answer, she just nodded her head in acknowledgement of her identity.

'I'm Detective Inspector Falconer from Market Darley CID, and this is my partner, Detective Sergeant Carmichael,' the inspector said by way of introduction. 'We've come in response to your 999 call.'

Miss Fairfield began to cry again, her body wracked by great hiccoughing sobs, as she remembered afresh what had happened. 'I-I'm s-so s-sorry. I just d-don't seem t-to be able t-to t-take it in,' she stuttered, between waves of tears. 'It all s-seems s-so unreal – like a d-dream – a n-nightmare.'

Carmichael immediately sat down beside her on the sofa, his giant frame dwarfing hers, and put a hand round her shoulders. 'Just let it all out,' he advised her, 'and then you'll feel a little better, and we can talk to you, and start to investigate what took place.'

At that juncture, Mrs Jenkins re-entered the room carrying a large, old-fashioned tray, and set it down on a low table that sat so conveniently for the sofa, and the two armchairs that comprised Mrs Jenkins' three-piece-suite, a dazzling affair in red, orange, and yellow velour.

As Mrs Jenkins poured tea for everyone, solicitously asking whether they took milk and sugar, Falconer gazed around him at the room in which they sat. Mrs Jenkins was evidently fond of bright colours, her three-piece-suite being a sufficient example of this to confirm such a belief. Just to add even more evidence to his surmise, the walls were hung with bright prints, and the two rugs on the floor also glowed with jewel-bright colours.

'Very nice, bright room,' he complimented her. Although he preferred more muted shades himself, he needed her on his side if he were to question Miss Fairfield without undue interruption and opposition. She must become an ally, not an enemy.

With the chocolate biscuits being handed round on a pretty porcelain plate, Carmichael removed himself from the sofa, Mrs Jenkins sat down comfortably beside Chelsea Fairfield, and Falconer took the spare armchair. There! That was them all settled now. He'd give it a couple more minutes for the tea and biscuits to do their job of soothing, then the questioning could begin.

Miss Fairfield was calmer now, and had accepted a cup of tea and a couple of biscuits with admirable dignity. Carmichael, without a shred of dignity at all, shoved a chocolate biscuit, whole, into his mouth, to free his hands to extract his notebook from his jacket pocket. To see his sergeant's mouth dealing with such a large offering was an experience Falconer rather wished he had not been witness to. The faces he was making made him look totally alien, and not a little half-witted.

Fortunately, neither of the women noticed, and Falconer only stared because he could not avert his fascinated eyes. They were glued to the spectacle, and there was not a thing he could do about it. Swallowing mightily, Carmichael smiled across at the inspector, and helped himself to another biscuit.

As the whole of it disappeared into his mouth again, Falconer pretended to be interested in the knick-knacks on the mantelpiece, to save himself a repeat of what he had witnessed before.

Chelsea Fairfield finally put down her cup and saucer, blew her nose quietly into the bundle of tissues she still had in her hand, and pulled herself into a bolt-upright sitting position, thus indicating that she was composed now and ready to talk.

Carmichael jammed a final biscuit into his gaping maw and sat with notepad and pen at the ready, but turned slightly away from the group, so that his activity would not be too intrusive and interrupt the natural flow of questioning.

Falconer opened the proceedings. 'Mr Standing – I believe that's the name you gave the desk sergeant? – Mr Malcolm Standing was your boyfriend?' he asked gently, starting with the easier-to-ask questions so as not to upset her too early in the process.

'Yes,' she whispered.

'And you had been going out with him for how long?'

'About three weeks.'

'And what were your plans for last night?' Falconer was gently approaching the nub of the matter.

'It was our first Valentine's Day together, and I wanted to make it really special.'

'In what way?' he probed, but he had obviously touched a sensitive spot, because her face crumpled into a grimace of misery.

'I was going to let him spend the night with me.' She spoke so quietly that he could hardly discern the words.

'And that would have been the first time that he had been invited to do so?' Falconer felt like a rat, poking and prying into this very private part of her life, but it was part of the job and had to be carried out and accepted for what it was.

'That's right,' Chelsea confirmed with a small nod of her head.

'So, what had you planned for the evening?'

'We were going to have some cocktails. They're not something I've ever really drunk before, but a couple of weeks ago I went out with a bunch of girls and we went to a club that specialised in them, and I thought it would be really romantic if we had some, to celebrate being together.'

'You're doing very well, Miss Fairfield,' Falconer praised her, then had his attention distracted by Carmichael, who was doubled over in his chair, coughing, biscuit crumbs flying everywhere.

'Sorry, guv,' he said, between coughs. 'Crumbs went down the wrong way.' Honestly, you could only ever take Carmichael anywhere twice; the second time to apologise.

Trying to recreate the intimate atmosphere that Carmichael had so thoroughly shattered, Falconer continued, 'And what cocktails did you drink?' This might have seemed a pointless question to some, but it could produce the key to the young man's death in that he may prove to have had a severe allergy to one of the ingredients.

'I had a White Lady, and he had a Sidecar.'

'And was it just the one drink?'

'Oh, no. We had more than one. It was such a special night, you see,' she explained. 'And we smoked Russian cigarettes. I wanted it to be so exotic and romantic, and as far away as it was possible to get from a night down at the pub.'

'I understand,' Falconer assured her. 'And who mixed the cocktails?'

'I did. I bought a book, so that I could get the recipes right. I even bought a cocktail shaker. No one in my family's ever had one of those before.' So, she was breaking new ground, socially.

'What happened, when you'd had your cocktails?' This was the difficult bit – finding out about how the young man had become ill, deteriorated, and finally lost his life.

'He said he felt funny, but I just thought it was the exotic drinks that he wasn't used to. Then he got sort of dizzy and unwell; said he felt awful, so I thought the best thing to do would be to settle him down on my sofa for the night, and see how he was in the morning. Of course, it ruined our romantic Valentine's night in, but that didn't matter.

'I got a blanket, and made him as comfortable as I could, then I – I went to bed. That sounds terribly callous, but I didn't think there was that much wrong with him. I thought it was just the strength of the cocktails. If I'd have known how serious it was, I'd have called a doctor. I'm so sorry. This is all my fault!'

'Of course it's not, Miss Fairfield. You're not medically trained. How on earth could you have known what the consequences would be?'

'I should have played safe and called for help,' she stated, tears now coursing down her cheeks. 'But I was woozy too. Cocktails seem to be much stronger than you think they're going to be. I just thought he was a bit more of a lightweight than me where alcohol was concerned, and staggered up to bed because my own head was spinning so much. So much for a romantic evening in! 'Oh, why didn't I call a bloody doctor'?' she wailed in despair, and Mrs Jenkins took her in her arms and rocked her like a baby.

'There, there, lovey. Don't take on so. There's no way anyone can turn back the clock, now is there? We just has to put up with what life dishes out to us, and make the best of it, don't we? Come on, lovey, pull yourself together. You were doin' marvellous there, givin' all that information to the nice inspector.

'Get a hold of yourself, now, and just answer the rest of his questions, then I'll put you upstairs in my own spare room, what used to be my Sharon's, and you can have a nice nap while everyone else gets on with finding out what happened to your poor old boyfriend.' Mrs Jenkins patted Chelsea on the back in a maternal fashion, and gently returned her to her upright position. 'There you are, my duck. Won't be long now, and I'll make you a nice cup of cocoa afore you goes up.'

Falconer had judged this neighbour well, for she was proving a tower of strength now, dealing with Chelsea Fairfield's explosions of emotion, and he was grateful to have been spared the job of doing it himself. Of course, Carmichael would have been better at it than he, he acknowledged, and, in reality, he would probably have left it to his sergeant to restore a calm atmosphere.

Chapter Three

15th February, – –later

The two detectives left Chelsea Fairfield in Mrs Jenkins' tender care and went round to take a look inside number twelve. Red and white crime tape sealed off the house at the path, and they ducked under it to approach the policeman on duty at the door, who had stood stoically silent as Mrs Jenkins had hopped, slightly arthritically, back and forth across the adjoining wall when they arrived.

'Good day to you, PC Proudfoot,' Falconer greeted him. 'Dr Christmas showed up yet?'

'Arrived just after you went in next door, sir,' answered PC John Proudfoot, drawing up his somewhat portly body into the best imitation of 'attention' he could manage. 'Photographer's been, and so has the fingerprint jonnie, sir. There're a couple of SOCOs waiting to see what you'd like them to do with regards to searching.'

Duty done, the constable lost his grip on his strenuously maintained upright position and slumped into a version of 'at ease'. His protruding belly just could not cope with being held in restraint for longer than a couple of minutes, and he thought he'd really have to cut down on the pork pies and Mars bars that he usually had about his person for emergency snacks.

Falconer and Carmichael entered the house, and Falconer couldn't help but notice the complete contrast in decor between this house and the neighbouring property. Where Mrs Jenkins filled her house with chaotic and eye-catching colour, this house was presented in muted shades, highlighted here and there with the addition of a couple of bright cushions or a single picture on a wall.

No bric-a-brac crowded shelves or mantelpiece, and the whole place, knocked through as it was into one large living, dining, and cooking space, was airy, light, and contemporary.

Mrs Jenkins' house looked like it had been furnished by someone who habituated market stalls and went on holiday to the more English resorts in Spain every year. Chelsea Fairfield's home, in contrast, looked as if its interior design had been culled from up-market magazines and such like. Falconer favoured neither look, but was nonetheless impressed with how very different two neighbouring homes with identical floor plans could look.

Fingerprints having been taken, they found Dr Christmas round the other side of the 'L' shape, washing his hands at the kitchen sink. 'Sorry about this,' he apologised, apropos of nothing. 'It's those damned gloves I have to wear. They leave an awful smell on my hands, and I can't wait to wash them as soon as I've taken the damned things off.'

'Hi there, Philip,' Falconer greeted him, having worked with the doctor a few times now, and managed to establish a congenial working relationship with him. 'Anything to tell us?'

'Apart from the fact that you've got a dead 'un, not really. To all intents and purposes, it would appear that he ingested something that disagreed with him, to the point of fatality. What that substance was I can't tell you at the moment.'

'Stomach contents?' queried the inspector.

'You've got it in one. Also, the fingerprints guy waltzed off with a couple of cocktail glasses and a cocktail shaker. I've rung for the meat wagon, to take the body to the mortuary, and I'll get him opened up as soon as I can. Do you want to sit in on this one?' he asked.

'Why not?' Falconer replied. 'We'll both keep you company,' he volunteered, pretending not to notice the greenish tinge that was colouring Carmichael's face at the very thought of attending a post mortem. 'I haven't attended one for ages – must be getting squeamish in my old age. What about you, Carmichael? When did you last attend an autopsy?'

Carmichael had to suppress the impulse to gag, before he managed to squeak, 'Just the once.'

'Well, it's time you widened your experience, my lad,' Dr Christmas commented hard-heartedly, totally unaware that Carmichael had a weak stomach and was liable to lose the contents of his own insides with remarkably little provocation. 'I'll get on with it first thing tomorrow morning, Harry. See you both at the mortuary at nine o'clock, sharp!'

As the doctor made his exit, the two remaining police personnel approached Falconer to receive instructions as to what they should be looking for. One of them took it upon himself, to be the first to speak. 'By the way, sir,' he began, addressing Falconer, 'we found the back door unlocked this morning. Maybe the young lady forgot to lock it, given the circumstances of her boyfriend being unwell, and feeling a little drunk herself.'

'Gadzooks!' Falconer exclaimed. 'The jungle drums round here are damned efficient. I've only just learnt all that myself, but thanks for the information. If it was unlocked all evening, it might not preclude the possibility that someone entered that way and put something in the cocktail shaker, or one of the bottles, because if Miss Fairfield and Mr Standing were round here, drinking, they wouldn't have been able to see the back door. The bottles will all have to go away for testing as well.'

'You don't think this could have been the work of the young lady then, sir?' asked the other officer.

'From what I've seen of her, I don't think so, but we must investigate all possibilities. When we've finished here and got everything nicely recorded at the station, Carmichael and I will go back next door and dig a little deeper into her background, and that of her boyfriend.

'I shall need a fingertip search done of the garden and any pathways. If anything was introduced into something that young man drank, then it had to be contained in something, so you'll be looking for a small discarded container of some kind. If it was glass, then maybe it was even ground underfoot. Pull out all the stops on this one, and don't forget the wheelie-bin's contents. Many a vital clue has been lost because no one fancied scrabbling through the contents of a refuse container. As it is, the local paper will probably lead tomorrow with the story, with a ghastly headline like "St Valentine's Day Massacre".

With a duet of 'yes, sirs', the two SOCOs went about their business, and the two detectives headed back to the police station to consolidate what they had learnt so far.

Having stopped for a drink, with a cup of coffee for Falconer and a huge mug of tea (with six sugars) for Carmichael, they chatted about matters unrelated to crime to give themselves a proper break.

'How are you finding married life, then, Carmichael?' Falconer asked, for Carmichael had married his sweetheart at New Year. 'I believe I've actually recovered from the wedding hangover now, but it's taken a long while.'

'You're pulling my leg, sir,' retorted Carmichael, more at ease with the inspector now than he had been when they had first been partnered together. 'And it's grand. I felt like I'd won the jackpot before when we were engaged, and I went over to spend the evenings with Kerry and the boys. Sometimes the Warren-Brownes would babysit, and we'd go out on a proper date. But being married? It's absolutely fantastic, sir. I'd recommend it to anyone.'

'So you quite like it, then?'

'Ha ha, sir. Very funny!'

'Any plans to add to the family?'

'!' Carmichael gave the inspector a very old-fashioned look, which was immediately understood.

'Of course, it's none of my business. I apologise for prying, Carmichael.'

'That's all right, sir, but you know how I feel about discussing anything ... like that.'

'I should have remembered.'

'How are your three cats getting on, sir? All well?'

'Very well, thank you. And all eating me out of house and home. Their latest little stunt must have been a joint effort, considering the strength needed to accomplish it. I got home one night a couple of weeks ago, and they'd managed to deposit the back half of a dead rabbit in the middle of the kitchen floor.'

'Half a rabbit?' Carmichael was dumbfounded.

'That's what I thought, until I realised it was probably one that had been run over on the main road, and they'd found it, just grabbed the best bit of booty on offer, and brought it home to me as a little present.'

'Makes a lovely stew or a pie,' said Carmichael, a faraway look in his eyes. 'One of my ma's treats for us when I was a nipper was a rabbit pie. One of my uncles used to go out lamping, and bring her back a brace now and again.'

'I don't think we want to pursue that line any further, Carmichael. I'd hate to have to arrest a member of your family for poaching.'

'Much appreciated, sir,' replied the sergeant, only now aware of what he had let slip.

'Well, better get our noses back to the grindstone. We've got to go back to Coronation Terrace before we're finished for the day, and I want to go to see someone from Standing's family too.'

Bob Bryant had managed to trace Malcolm Standing's next-of-kin, and PC Green had been dispatched to break the news of his death, a job Falconer had hated doing in the past, when it had fallen to his lot. It was the worst news you could bring to anyone, and it always made him feel like an absolute heel having to be the one to break it. He and Carmichael therefore had the address of Mr and Mrs David Standing with them, so that they could pay a visit after returning to Coronation Terrace to continue their questioning of Chelsea Fairfield.

She was up and about, having woken about a quarter of an hour before they arrived, and was now having a cup of tea at Mrs Jenkins' kitchen table. She looked less panic-stricken and upset than she had before when she turned to greet them, and Falconer considered that she had only been going out with the young man for three weeks, and they had not yet instigated a physical relationship. Maybe she'd get over it quicker than he'd thought when he saw her earlier.

At their arrival, Ida Jenkins hurriedly produced two more cups and saucers and poured tea for her two new visitors. As Carmichael ladled sugar into his, she remarked, 'I've never seen anyone take his tea that sweet before, Sergeant Carmichael. But then, you do have a big frame to maintain, so I expects you needs it.' Carmichael just smiled at her, and continued to spoon a little more sugar into his already sticky brew.

Falconer courteously finished his cup of tea before announcing that it was time they resumed questioning. 'I need to know a little more about you and the deceased,' (he winced at the harsh reality of the word) 'Miss Fairfield. I know this is painful for you, so soon after the event, but it is necessary, I assure you.'

'I do understand, and once I've told you, it's done, so fire away, Inspector.' replied Chelsea.

'I need to know, and this may seem a little odd, where you work, and where Mr Standing worked. I would also like you to tell me how and where you met, and anything you know about his life before he met you.'

'I work in the pharmacy in the High Street, and Malcolm ... worked,' (she had a little trouble using the past tense, in this reference to him) 'as a sous chef in the Italian restaurant, about three doors from the pharmacy. We worked so close together, but never came across each other until recently,' she informed the two detectives, Carmichael huddled over his notebook, his chair pulled to a slight remove from the table so as not to draw attention to his note-taking.

'Did he tell you anything about his past, or his family?'

'Not a lot. He just said he'd worked there for a few years, and that he was estranged from his family. I never met any of them.'

'Did he say why?' This had interested Falconer.

At this question, she flicked her eyes away from the table and took a deep breath. 'We never discussed it,' she answered abruptly.

'What, never?' Falconer was definitely interested.

'He said he didn't want to talk about it: that it had been some silly adolescent squabble, and that it wasn't relevant to his life anymore. I took him at his word.'

'Do you know where his family lives?'

'I'm afraid not,' Chelsea answered, shaking her head to emphasise this negative.

'Did he have brothers and sisters?'

'I've no idea,' she said, again shaking her head.

'You really knew very little about him, then,' Falconer stated.

'People's pasts don't concern me; only their presents and futures,' she stated emphatically, as if this were really important to her.

'But surely what has happened to us makes us who we are today'?' commented the inspector.

Chelsea's answer consisted of just two words, 'Not necessarily,' and then she clamped her mouth shut, and stared down at the table blankly.

'I think we'll leave it there for now, thank you, Miss Fairfield. We'll be in touch when we have any more news or information. Thank you for your time, and thank you again, Mrs Jenkins, for the refreshments.'

They rose to leave but, just as they were passing through the kitchen door, Falconer looked back and caught a sideways glance after them that expressed extreme relief, on Chelsea Fairfield's face. It could just be a normal reaction. It could be that she was concealing something. He didn't know which, but he intended to find out.

Chapter Four

16th February

In the office the next morning, Falconer and Carmichael fell into a casual chat as they waited for various pieces of information to filter through to them which would allow them to continue their investigation.

'Buying that cottage next door to Kerry's was the best thing I ever did,' Carmichael threw out casually.

'It was originally bought by a couple of weekenders, wasn't it, after that first case we worked together?' asked Falconer.

'That's right, sir. With two very noisy dogs. I don't think the Brigadier knew what had hit him when they bought it. He did nothing but complain to them when they were down for the weekend, and even went to the Parish Council to see if anything could be done about it, but they said he'd just have to put up with it or get the noise abatement officer in from the council if he wanted to take it any further.'

'So they didn't settle?' Falconer had never heard the full story, and was in just the right sort of mood to have his mind distracted while he waited. 'They can't have felt very welcome. I've met the Brigadier, and he can be a fearsome character.'

'They only came down for a few weekends. Kerry left it as it was, telling them that she'd been through it, and they could keep anything they thought was of any interest to them, but the state of the place just defeated them.

'Not only was there a tremendous amount of work to do, but they had constant complaints about their dogs barking, and there was nothing to do in the village, and only the village pub and the tea-shop to amuse them.

'They soon got fed up with spending every weekend they came down clearing out and cleaning, and when Kerry and I had a talk about it, and I offered to buy it from them at the price they'd paid for it, they jumped at the chance.

'Kerry and I knew we'd get married even then, so it seemed like an ideal opportunity for me to take out a mortgage and buy the place, so that we could enlarge the living quarters, without all the upheaval of having to move. And with me buying it, it left Kerry's nest-egg intact for anything big that came up in the future. It was a form of being joined together before we actually tied the knot.'

'Smart move, Carmichael. So now *you've* got to do all the clearing out and renovation.'

'No problem, sir. One of my brothers has got a flat-bed truck, so it'll be easy to get all the rubbish to the tip, and everyone in my family's a dab-hand with a paint brush. We'll get there, and it's a bit of an adventure, too, all the funny little personal bits and pieces we come across, and all the old photos.'

'So, life's being good to you at the moment, Carmichael?' asked Falconer.

'It's just got better and better, since we've worked together,' Carmichael stated, without a whit of embarrassment.

'You soppy old sentimentalist, you!' said Falconer, nevertheless feeling pleased. They did work well together, chalk and cheese that they were, and he was beginning to feel proud of the partnership they were forging.

The telephone rang on Falconer's desk, and as he answered the call, Carmichael applied himself to his computer to carry out the check he'd promised himself he'd do first thing this morning, and had then been waylaid from his intended task by his enthusiasm for his new-found happiness.

Placing the telephone to his ear, a voice spoke without preamble. 'Get your lazy-ass butts over here now! You promised me you'd both attend the post-mortem, and I'm not starting it without *both* of you being here in person.'

He realised immediately that it was Dr Christmas, and blushed at being so remiss. Not only had he forgotten all about their agreement the day before, but it seemed, so had Carmichael. 'I'm so sorry. We both seemed to have suffered a crisis in short-term memory. We'll be over as soon as we can,' he apologised, and ended the call, indicating to Carmichael that they were going out.

'Just a minute, sir. I've got something here!'

'Can't it wait?'

'No, I don't think it can. I've just run Malcolm Standing through the records, and although he has no criminal convictions, it would seem he received a police caution in 2005,' Carmichael informed him.

'What for? Anything interesting?' asked Falconer.

'Don't know if it's relevant, sir, but I don't think it shows him up in a very satisfactory light,' said Carmichael. 'He was cautioned for interfering with a little girl – not very edifying – and it would appear that it wasn't just a one-off offence.'

'We'll see what we can dig up later,' offered Falconer, continuing, 'We haven't got time to do anything about it now. That was Christmas on the phone. We've both forgotten about his blasted post mortem. We were supposed to be there first thing, remember?'

'Oh no!' groaned Carmichael, turning pale. 'I'd completely forgotten about that.'

'So had I, but good old Dr Christmas has stayed his scalpel, until we arrive. Aren't we the lucky bunnies then?'

'No, sir,' disagreed the sergeant, reluctantly following the inspector out of the office, and on their way to an event that both of them would rather have been spared.

Market Darley was too small a town to have its own mortuary, so any bodies in need of storage or a post mortem were kept at the hospital mortuary, and it was in this direction that Harry Falconer drove his beloved Boxster now. Carmichael, beside him in the passenger seat, was unusually quiet, and Falconer enquired if he was all right.

'Not really, sir. I've got a rather delicate stomach.'

'What, with a physique like yours?'

'Can't help it. I've always been like it.'

'Well, I expect Dr Christmas will have the odd bowl or bucket lying around, should you need one. He's always got things like that on hand, for the various bits and pieces he removes from the bodies.'

'Gee, thanks, sir! And I had a really good fry-up this morning, too,' replied Carmichael in a sepulchral voice.

At the hospital, Dr Christmas was already scrubbed-up, gowned, and gloved, practically trembling with his eagerness to wield his various knives, saws, and maybe even a chisel or two. He enjoyed a great deal of Schadenfreude from observing others observing him carrying out this routine task.

Their reactions were so different, and he could never predict who would be sick, who would pass out cold, and who would just observe, and take an intelligent interest, without any reaction at all, to the various bits that were usually on the inside of a body, being delivered, like bastard deformed creatures, to the outside. Sometimes he'd have a little bet with himself, but he hardly ever won. There was nowt so queer as folk, in his opinion.

Falconer heartily disliked seeing people sliced and diced, as if they were in some sort of bizarre cannibal kitchen, but he could cope with it, because of what he had experienced on active duty in the army.

Carmichael was not quite so worldly-wise, and was unusually squeamish when it came to a lot of substances – inside things being outside, blood, and bones being three of them. He also could not deal with vomit, but predicted that it would only be his own that upset his stomach today.

It was the great Y-shaped cut that set Carmichael off: that and the cutting of the ribs to reveal the contents of the chest cavity. Taking a few steps back from the proceedings, he bent nearly double and gave an enormous heave. Dr Christmas's assistant was more than prepared, however, and managed to pop a bucket under his mouth just before a great whoosh of breakfast sprayed out of the sergeant's mouth.

'Ups-a-daisy!' this anonymous individual encouraged him, and stood there stolidly until the gauge on Carmichael's stomach was registering 'empty'. This was all carried out as quietly as possible, as Dr Christmas was speaking into a small suspended microphone, as he noted his findings.

Carmichael was led solicitously away, and settled down somewhere where he could not see what was being carried out, before being offered a large mug of heavily-sugared tea to settle his stomach.

He was just finishing this, and feeling a shade more human, when Falconer and Dr Christmas entered the room, both of them looking perfectly well and not the slightest bit wobbly. 'Please don't discuss it while I'm here,' he begged them. 'If you want to talk about, I'd rather go outside and get some air, and wait for you there.'

'I'll be there in a few minutes,' Falconer assured him, and he left them to their post-post mortem discussion.

Carmichael sat himself down on the boundary wall of the little mortuary car park, and sucked in mouthful after mouthful of clean, living air, and Falconer, true to his word, joined him within ten minutes. In his hand he held an empty carrier bag, which he handed to Carmichael. 'Here you are!' he said.

'What's that for?' asked Carmichael.

'To keep under your mouth on the drive back to the station. After this start to the day, if we go out again, we'll take your car. I will not tolerate you being sick in my Boxster, and that's that! If you're sick at the wheel of your own car, I'll happily hold the bag over the steering wheel for you, but I will not allow even the chance of you 'chucking up' in my beauty.'

Back at the station, Falconer had a word with Bob Bryant about the information that Carmichael had turned up on the computer before they had been peremptorily summoned to the mortuary. 'This dead chap, Bob,' he explained. 'Name of Malcolm Standing. It seems he received a caution for child abuse in 2005, when he was in his early twenties. I wondered if there was anything you could dig out about it for me.'

'Seems to ring a bell, but I don't know if the details will be on the computer yet,' Bob answered, his expression one of careful thought. 'I'll see what I can dig up – or get dug up – for you. I'll also ask around, see if anyone remembers it, or was involved. I'll send up anything I find to you, 'ASAP.'

'Thanks, Bob. I owe you one.' If you wanted to know anything about past cases, or even police gossip, you consulted Bob Bryant, who seemed to have worked on the desk forever, and knew every little thing that happened, as if it reached out to him from the past out of the ether.

Upstairs in the office, he found Carmichael sprawled backwards in his chair, still an unnatural colour, and insisted his sergeant took an early lunch, as his tank was obviously out of fuel, and he wouldn't be able to think straight without it. Carmichael smiled at him wanly and ambled off, still looking unhappy, in search of nourishment and a happier tummy.

Chapter Five

15th February – afternoon

When Carmichael returned to the office, he looked a lot more like his normal self and, as Falconer had just stopped to eat his own healthy lunch – a box of salad and a wholemeal bap, followed by an apple and a banana – he took the opportunity to find out a little more about Carmichael's family, the members of which he had met at the sergeant's and Kerry's wedding at the very beginning of the year, but had been rather 'blurred' at the time, and he was now unable to recall them very clearly.

'Well, there's six of us,' Carmichael started. 'Four boys and two girls.'

'And where do you come in that order?' Falconer enquired.

'I'm the fourth and last boy, then come my two sisters.'

'And their names – all of them?'

'My oldest brother's called Romeo, but everybody calls him 'Rome'. He's a builder. Gave me a bit of a hand when I built my little hideaway, when I lived at home. Then there's Hamlet – I told you my ma had this Shakespearian thing about names. He's known as Ham, and he works on a farm.

'Number three is Mercutio – just called Merc, like the car. He's a sort of 'man with a van'. He does small removals, house clearance, odd jobs, and gardening. He reckons the variety of jobs is good for him and stops him getting bored. Then it's me, but you know about me, because we work together,' said Carmichael, stating the bleedin' obvious. 'I got the Ralph bit, because my ma was really taken with an actor at the time – some fellow called Richardson.'

'Tell me, Carmichael, is your 'ma'' (Falconer suppressed a wince at this mode of maternal address) 'a great Shakespeare fan, then?'

'Not really. She just liked the names he used in his plays. Said they had a sort of 'ring' to them, like, but I'd better finish my family run-down.

'Next come the two girls. Juliet's the elder, and she's a hairdresser and beautician. Then, finally, there's Imogen, who's a librarian. She's done really well, passing all her exams and everything, and we're all very proud of her.'

'I should think they're all very proud of you, too,' Falconer commented.

'Yes, well, sort of,' replied Carmichael.

'What do you mean, sort of?' asked Falconer, not quite understanding why his family should not be really happy about what he was doing.

'Not everyone likes having a member of 'the fuzz' in their immediate family,' the sergeant stated baldly, turning slightly red, and avoiding Falconer's gaze.

''Nuff said, Carmichael. No further explanation needed or sought,' Falconer added, hoping to dispel the younger man's evident embarrassment, as he remembered the uncle who used to go out 'lamping' for rabbits. That was, no doubt, one of his more innocent pastimes. What he didn't know couldn't hurt him, and he'd pry no further. 'What about your parents? How did they cope with such a large brood?' 'Dad's a lot older than Ma. He's retired now, but he used to be a bus driver, then a coach driver. He always said he liked the long continental coach trips, 'cos at least it gave him the security of knowing that he couldn't get Ma in pod again while he was away. He swears that most of us kids were conceived just from him kissing her goodbye on the cheek when he went to work in the mornings.

'Ma married him at sixteen, in a bit of a hurry, and she's never had a proper, paid job. She said she always had too much to do just keeping house and home together, and preventing us kids from overthrowing western society, but I think she was joking about that last bit,' he concluded.

'I should hope so!' exclaimed Falconer, trying to digest the plethora of facts he had just been offered. By crikey! He bet their Christmases were good, if Carmichael's wedding had been anything to go by. He just hoped that he was never asked to join their celebrations.

'Ma says that after six kids, her pelvic floor's so riddled with woodworm, that if one more kid trod on it, they'd go right through,' Carmichael added as an afterthought, and Falconer wrinkled his nose in disgust, determined to change the subject at all costs. He had no wish whatsoever to learn anything further about Mrs Carmichael senior's insides, having just had an intimate encounter with those of Malcolm Standing that morning.

'And how are the two little dogs you got last month? I'm sorry, I can't remember their names offhand.'

'Fang and Mr Knuckles,' declaimed Carmichael with pride, suitably distracted. Fang was a Chihuahua puppy, and Mr Knuckles a miniature Yorkshire terrier. When Falconer had first seen them they were tiny balls of fluff, which looked ridiculous cradled by the enormous Carmichael.

'They're getting on great! The boys love them, and they get more walks than they can cope with, poor little things. They slot right into the family, as if a gap has been waiting for them for some time. You must come and visit them sometime, sir.'

'We'll see, Carmichael. Not when we're in the middle of an investigation.'

Later that afternoon, Bob Bryant came upstairs with a dog-eared buff folder for Falconer, this being the file on Malcolm Standing's official caution. 'There were, apparently, some newspaper cuttings supposed to be in here, too, but they seem to have gone missing. I know there was a bit of a fuss about it at the time.

'We don't know who leaked it to the press, but that's the sort of thing that happens when it's a case of interfering with little kids. People get upset and can't bear to see it brushed under the carpet, even if there's no court case or prosecution,' he explained, having handed over the slim folder.

'Thanks for that, Bob. I'll have a little read of this, see if it throws any light on anything.'

There was very little in the case notes to help, but there were references on a separate sheet of paper to local newspaper reports which sensationalised the caution, blowing it out of all proportion and demonising the young Malcolm Standing.

It had all been five years ago now, and the dust must have settled, as Malcolm had been in the last job he was ever to hold for three years. It made him think of something someone had said when he was a child, and which had impressed itself on his memory, although he didn't completely understand it at the time. 'Good times, bad times, all times pass over.'

This sensation of its time had also passed over, and allowed the younger Standing to get whatever it was that had driven him to it out of his system, and try to lead a more normal life thereafter.

Many of Falconer's dealings with the local press in the past had been with the *Carsfold Gazette*, but this had happened in Market Darley and, after checking the telephone number, he put through a call to the *Market Darley Post* – a local newspaper that was more likely to have carried the story – asking for the editor when his call was answered.

'Good morning. I am Detective Inspector Falconer from Market Darley CID, and I was wondering if I could have a rummage through your archives for some information that may be pertinent to a case I'm working on at the moment?' he asked.

'Good morning, Chief Inspector Falconer. My name's Garry Mathers – that's two 'r's in Garry – and I should be delighted to be of assistance to the constabulary, provided, of course, that I get a scoop on whatever story is about to break.'

'Typical press!' thought Falconer, before replying, 'There might not be any case to break, but whatever comes of it, I promise that you will be the first to know. Is it all right if I pop over now? Time is always rather pressing during an investigation.'

'No problemo, squire! I am here to serve my community.'

Oh boy! He had a feeling he wasn't going to like this, but it had to be done.

Half an hour later found Falconer sitting in a back room at the offices of the *Market Darley Post*, scrolling through records of back numbers of the newspaper. Garry Mathers had provided him with the relevant year, and he knew the date of the official caution, so he worked from that date onwards, scrutinising each issue with a view to identifying any and every paragraph about Malcolm Standing's misdemeanour.

It seemed that the local press had made rather a large meal of the event, and headlines proclaimed the presence in the streets of Market Darley of a young and dangerous paedophile, stalking his victims at will, and, as yet, not behind bars. There were follow-up articles about the public outcry, and a special double-page letters section, allowing the town's residents to have their say, and it didn't make pleasant reading.

There was mention of another child being questioned about whether she had been assaulted or approached by Standing, but her (it was made obvious that this was a 'she') name was never mentioned. The identity of the child, concerning whom the caution had been issued, was also not published for legal reasons, so the articles were not a great deal of help to him. All they really did was to clarify the public hostility the young man must have endured at the time, and how difficult it must have been for him to live this down and start afresh, trying to live a more normal life after all the publicity had been superseded by more current events.

He'd rather naively pinned his hopes on learning something from this outdated reportage, forgetting that the young victim of any sort of abuse was guaranteed anonymity, and he supposed he must have hoped that someone would have let a name 'slip' at the time. Even if they had, the newspaper had not had the temerity to print it, no doubt fearing prosecution should they have done so.

Before he left, he even sought out Garry (with two 'r's!) in his office, to see if he could give him a name on the Q.T. but that was no-go, either. He'd only been there a year, and had no knowledge of events in Market Darley that long ago. 'I moved down from Town,' he explained. 'Thought I'd rather be a big fish in a small pond, than a minnow in the shark-infested waters of the capital.'

So, that was that! Dead end! What now? He decided to go back to Bob Bryant, and see what he could winkle out of the darker corners of his memory.

'Anything you can drag up, Bob,' he pleaded with the desk sergeant, as he entered the station, after his abortive treasure hunt.

'Leave it with me, and I'll give you a tinkle as soon as anything comes back to me,' he promised, and Falconer had to be content with that.

When he got back to his own office, he found a message to contact Dr Christmas, an activity he carried out without delay. He might have identified the substance that caused Standing's death, and that might give them a clue as to who had administered it. Although Chelsea Fairfield was the obvious choice, she had not struck him as a murderer, and Malcolm Standing had had a lot of enemies from the past.

He was in luck, as Christmas answered on the third ring. 'Hello there, Harry. I've got some news for you, my boy.' Bingo! And the doctor sounded happy, so it looked like Falconer was finally going to learn something solid about the case.

'The lab's identified what that young chap ingested. You'll never guess what it was.'

'Don't tease me, please. I can hardly stand the suspense,' Falconer pleaded.

'It was a whacking great dose of good old-fashioned valium. If that girl had called for help when he first started feeling strange, they could have saved him, but valium is a muscle relaxant, and it works on the chest muscles as well and suppresses breathing. If she'd have summoned an ambulance, they could have got him pumped out and stabilised him. As it was, he died of suffocation.'

'I don't really know that I want to tell her that,' Falconer replied. 'She's worried enough about whether he would have been all right if she'd called a doctor the night before. This news would probably destroy her.'

'I'll leave that particular moral dilemma with you. My job is just to identify the cause of death, and pass on that information. Good luck!'

'Thanks, Philip. Goodbye.' Falconer put down the telephone, now faced with a new problem: to tell, or not to tell, that was the question.

While he was mulling this over, the internal phone system trilled, and he found Bob Bryant on the other end of the line. 'So soon?' he queried, knowing that Bob would know what he was talking about.

'I just remembered who administered the official caution, and you're not going to believe this, but it was our very own darling Superintendent 'Jelly' Chivers. It was just before he was promoted from detective chief inspector, and he must have frightened seven shades of shite out of that young lad, for he never reoffended, as far as I know.'

'Language, Bob!'

'I know, but put yourself in the lad's position. Yes, you've done something terrible, and now here you are in front of this terrifying monster while he roars the caution at you and delivers a hell-fire and brimstone lecture to you at the same time. I bet he wished the earth would open up and swallow him.'

'That doesn't detract from the seriousness of the matter, though, Bob,' Falconer felt compelled to point out.

'I realise that, but I bet if he was used on young offenders of any sort, he'd be a better deterrent than these soft Youth Detention Centres they put them in nowadays. I'd be willing to bet that anyone who's ever been cautioned by old Jelly has never reoffended, nor even considered it.' This was Bob Bryant's personal opinion, and nothing would sway him from his belief.

'You could be right, at that, Bob,' agreed Falconer, imagining how he'd felt in the past, when Chivers had given him a good bawling-out over something.

'So I've booked an appointment for you to see the great man himself, at 9.30 tomorrow morning.'

'Thanks a bunch, Bob. Do I get a last request before I enter his office, like a man facing a firing squad?'

'I should advise you to step warily. He's going to a golf club dinner tonight, and he's liable to have a sore head.'

'Great! So, not long after I get in tomorrow, I have to enter the den of a bear with a sore head, and try to get him to think back to something that happened five years ago?'

'That's about the size of it, Harry. Good luck! And let me see the wounds afterwards, won't you?'

Falconer finished the call with just one word, 'Rat!' but he heard Bob Bryant's chuckle. before the line went dead.

<u>Chapter Six</u>

16th February

The next morning, having dressed and carried out his daily grooming with especial care, Falconer found himself outside Superintendent Chivers' office with thirty seconds to spare. Counting them down conscientiously on his watch, he mouthed, 'Three, two, one,' and raised his hand to rap on the door when it unexpectedly opened, and he found himself apparently brandishing a fist in the superintendent's face.

'Sorry, sir,' he mumbled in apology, letting his hand drop.

'I was just coming out to see where the devil you'd got to,' snapped Chivers, striding back into his office and throwing himself, like a large sack of potatoes, into his chair. 'What do you want?'

'I need to talk to you about an official caution you delivered about five years ago,' Falconer began, only to be nearly blasted out of his socks by the voice of a volcano.

'Five years ago? How the devil am I supposed to remember something I did five years ago? Are you mad, man?'

'I think you'll remember this one, sir,' Falconer suggested humbly, glad that he hadn't been flattened in the blast. 'It concerns a young man called Malcolm Standing, and you were dealing with a case of interfering with a little girl. The parents didn't want to put their daughter through the trauma of a trial, I presume, but the press got hold of it somehow, and created a nine days' sensation out of it.'

Chivers sat in silence for a few seconds, then, it seemed, from his expression, that light had dawned. 'I do remember that one. Nasty business, very nasty indeed. I gave the little toe-rag a right dressing down, and it left me feeling physically sick to think what he'd done.'

'It's just that I need to know as much as I can about who was involved, with reference to a case I'm working on now. Standing has been murdered, and I wondered if it could have been done by someone connected with his misdemeanour back then.'

'I see,' said Chivers, thoughtfully. 'The child's family name was, I seem to remember, Ifield. She was their only child, Eileen, who was sinned against. She was thirteen when it finally came out. I don't know what the catalyst was, but she suddenly confessed to her mother, and it would seem that the abuse had been going on from when she was just seven years old until the previous year.'

'Is it possible that you still have an address for the Ifields? I'd like to speak to them, and to Eileen, about Standing. I wouldn't normally rake up something like this, but I need to catch whoever murdered him.'

'I'm afraid you're out of luck with all the members of the family. Mr and Mrs Ifield moved away from the area after their daughter committed suicide a couple of years ago.'

'She killed herself?' Falconer asked, aghast.

'That's right, and only sixteen years of age,' replied Superintendent Chivers, a shadow passing across his expression, as he remembered the sad event.

'How did she do it, sir?'

'With tablets. Something the doctor had prescribed for her. It was all that little bastard's doing, you know. She was never the same after that, her parents told me. I went to the funeral. Felt I had to; show some respect, and the support of the police.'

'I don't suppose you know what tablets she used, or who her doctor was at the time, sir?' Falconer was determined that there was a connection, and he wanted to get to the bottom of it.

'That I can't recall, but it was reported in the local paper. It might be worth your while trawling through their back issues for 2008. I seem to remember that they made a bit of a song and dance about it. Poor little abused girl, couldn't forget and get on with her life – you know the sort of melodramatic crap the media churn out. 'Probably hoped to start off the same old witch hunt again, but the general opinion seemed to be to let the past rest in peace. Raking it all up again wouldn't bring her back, or restore her innocence.

'We had a few calls from members of the public, asking us why we hadn't locked him up and thrown away the key, but I put out a press statement, informing them that the poor girl's life would have been even more blighted by having to go through the trauma of a court case. That soon shut them up. Sorry I can't be of more help, Harry.'

'You've been very helpful indeed. I'll drop in at the *Market Darley Post* offices, and have a look at 2008; see what they reported at the time of her suicide.'

'Good man. And good luck!'

Returning once more in the back room of the local newspaper offices, Falconer metaphorically shook himself free of the invisible slime that Garry Mathers had seemed to coat him in when he had first arrived, then set to work to hunt out the articles he was after.

It didn't take him long to find them, for the story had made the front page: the press, as usual, braying for someone's blood, and not caring in this case whether it came from the local constabulary or Malcolm Standing himself.

Reading the articles written at that time, and the statement issued by Chivers himself, he finally, just out of idle curiosity, began to hunt for the death notices of the young girl, or perhaps he should refer to her as a young woman, at sixteen years of age?

These he found without difficulty. Many of her friends and relatives had put separate announcements in, and he scanned the column conscientiously, his eyes widening with surprise as he read the last announcement, hardly able to believe what he was seeing.

With an expression of infinite sadness in his eyes, he packed up his notebook and left the building, towards the inevitable end of this case.

Back at the office once more, he collected Carmichael and requested that PC Linda 'Twinkle' Starr accompany him on his mission. To neither of them did he say anything, just asking them to take their lead from him, and follow standard police procedure.

He drove, and it wasn't long before they stopped outside Coronation Terrace. Number twelve was their destination, and his steps were slow and heavy as he walked up the garden path. PC Starr accompanied him: Carmichael had been instructed to go round to the back of the property, in case there was a last-minute escape attempt.

Chelsea Fairfield answered the door, her face a picture of panic and despair when she saw who was waiting for her. She'd been a great little actress up till now, but she realised the game was up.

'I think you know why we're here, don't you, Miss Fairfield?' Falconer asked, his voice thick with emotion at the waste of another young life.

'You'd better come in,' she said, as if she cared what the neighbours would think!

When Carmichael was alerted that they had gained entrance, he went next door to number ten and asked Mrs Jenkins to join them. She would be support for Chelsea in her hour of need, and she also made exceedingly good tea. If he was lucky, she might even bring some biscuits round with her. No matter how grave the circumstances, Carmichael was always hungry!

But Ida Jenkins went one better, and appeared at the front door with a cake tin. 'Just a little something I made yesterday,' she announced. 'Nothing like a bit of sugar to make you feel a bit stronger when times is trying, is there?' she asked of no one in particular.

She bustled around in the kitchen area in Chelsea's, clattering crockery and boiling the kettle, while Falconer got on with what he had come here for.

'Why did you do it?' he asked the young woman, who had not yet shed a tear at their discovery of her crime.

'She told me about what Malcolm had done when she was about eleven,' she said. 'And I told her that she had to do something about it, but she said she couldn't tell her mum. I used to go and stay there for a while, in the summer holidays, because we were both only children and they lived out of town. It didn't matter about the age difference: she was like a little sister to me.

'The next year, when I went back, I found out it was still going on and I was furious. Of course, by then, I wasn't staying there for long in the summer. I was seventeen years old, and I'd discovered boys and parties and I wanted to be with people my own age. Young people can be so selfish,' she finished, not noting the irony that she was still one of those young people. Maybe she'd had to grow up faster than most, though.

'I didn't want to get involved, but I asked her to show me where he lived, and I wrote him an anonymous letter telling him I'd castrate him if he ever laid a finger on her again, and it seemed that he did stop, but it was also me that told her parents she had something disturbing to tell them, and that they'd better get her to talk to them.

'Time went by so fast that we hardly spoke again until just before she took her own life. I think she'd discovered boys, and found that what he'd done to her had changed her. She didn't think she'd ever be able to have a boyfriend like normal girls do. It was all so sad. She'd lost so much weight. She used to be a chubby, laughing little child, but by the end, she looked like a skeleton. *He* did that to her!

'For me, it was over when I sent that letter and he left her alone, but it had haunted her ever since. As soon as I heard what she'd done, I went over there to see Auntie Maureen and Uncle Brian, and that's when I did it.'

'Did what?' Falconer asked her, his voice muted, his face careworn.

'I took the tablets she hadn't taken.'

'So it wasn't something you got from the pharmacy where you work?' Falconer asked.

'No. I took what was available at the time, and just hung on to them, because I decided there and then that I'd hunt that evil bastard down and somehow get even for her. And that's exactly what I did. Of course, I had to get on with my own life. Then I had to find him, and strike up some sort of relationship with him. Perhaps now you'll understand why I kept him waiting for you-know-what!

'I can't tell you how unbearable it felt, to have that creep slobbering all over me, and trying to get into my knickers for those three weeks.

'There was no way I was ever going to go to bed with that evil little pervert, but I was going to deliver justice to him – a life for a life!'

'Did you know what those tablets would do to him?' Falconer interjected at this juncture.

'I knew what they'd done to my cousin, and I just wanted the same thing to happen to him. I ground them up with my pestle and mortar, and dissolved them as best as I could before he arrived, then I split the suspension between two drinks, hurrying him through the first one so that I could get him to drink the second one before he lost consciousness.

'Of course, when I saw the reality of what I'd done, and phoned the station, I really was hysterical. I couldn't believe it! The seriousness of actually taking a life. But later, I remembered all that poor little Eileen had gone through, and I was glad.'

Her voice trailed off into silence, and Mrs Jenkins erupted into that silence, carrying a tray, and carolling, 'Tea and cake for everybody. Just the thing to lift the spirits, that's what I always say.'

THE END

Battered To Death

DI Falconer and DS Carmichael are both enjoying a well-earned rest day, when they are summoned to a most distressing incident that has occurred at a chip shop on the parade of shops in Upper Darley.

It was obviously murder, but was it something to do with the robust behaviour of some of the more aggressive customers from the night before or was it closer to home?

PORTION ONE

<u>Friday 16th April</u>

It was after ten o'clock on a mild evening, and the rather pathetically-named shop unit called Chish and Fips was doing its usual roaring trade for a Friday night. The shop was packed with customers being served and waiting to be served, with even one or two customers standing outside, waiting for the queue to get a little shorter, so that they could join it on the other side of the door.

The heat in the little unit was furnace-like, the faces of the customers nearest to the counter a bright red as the fryers belched out heat and clouds of steam. From outside, the little unit was a beacon of smeared colours, like a work of abstract art, behind its condensation-clouded and dripping plate-glass window. The face behind the counter, trying to cope on its own, was of a similar hue to that of its closest customers, but with the features down-turned and cross. The owner, Frank Carrington, had promised to come in at half-past nine to give her a hand, and had still not shown up.

'Who's next?' queried the cross-faced figure, Sylvia Beeton by name, trying to serve, wrap orders, rescue cooked food from the fryers, take money, give change, and put fresh food on to fry, all at the same time, and getting mighty fed-up with the gargantuan effort she was putting in for what was just a smidgen over the minimum wage.

As a voice shouted out for two cod and chips, and to make it quick, she shouted back, without diverting her gaze in the voice's direction, 'You wait your turn like everyone else, Sanjeev Khan. Just because your dad's on the council doesn't give you priority over anyone else.'

'Two cod and chips, one double battered sausage and chips, and one meat and potato pie and chips,' the next customer called out, while she was still adding up two burgers and chips, two pickled onions, a pineapple fritter, and a portion of chicken with extra chips.

'I'll be with you as soon as I can. I've only got one pair of hands, and I've not taken for this lot yet, she called out, handing over a bulging carrier bag and taking, in exchange, a high denomination note. 'Haven't you got anything smaller, sir?' she asked. 'Oh, well, can't be helped.' She sighed, then raised her voice to the rest of the gaggle in the shop, 'Correct money if you can, or as near as possible. I'm not a bank, and I've nearly run out of change. If you can't, I may have to refuse to serve you.'

As she got on with serving the next order, throwing an extra load of chips into the fryer and pulling a dozen pieces of fish out of the batter tray and throwing them into another receptacle of boiling fat (for everything was fried in lard in this establishment, in the old-fashioned way), there was a muttering amongst the customers, and some, who knew each other, got wallets out and rummaged around in pockets to see if they had the exact money, or could help out friends, who looked woebegone, when they flashed a twenty-pound note at them, and felt devastated at possibly having to forego their supper just because of lack of change.

The queue shortened slowly, as the lull before 'chucking-out' time at the pubs arrived and from the flat upstairs there suddenly boomed an almighty racket of drum and bass music, shaking the fluorescent light fitting on the ceiling and causing some customers to cover their ears.

'It's all right,' Sylvia shouted. 'I'll just go up and give them a blasting. I can't take orders with this racket going on,' and with that, she was off, through a door at the back, and could be heard thumping up a flight of stairs to the first floor. There was then a roar that rose even above the music, the deafening racket was turned down to a reasonable volume, and Sylvia returned, a look of triumph on her face.

'That's sorted *them* out!' she said, with satisfaction, rubbing her plump hands together with satisfaction. 'Now, who's next? Curry Khan, you put that can of drink back in the fridge where it belongs. If I know you, you'll high-tail off with it before I get to your order. You can take one then, and not before.'

'But I'm thirsty, Mrs Beeton.'

'Then squeeze to the front and put the exact money on the counter, and I'll let you take it now, and then you can wait for your order like everybody else here. But no pay, no drink. Got it?'

'Got it, Ma,' agreed Curry, the son of the owner of the local Indian restaurant, and leaned through and put a pound piece on the serving bar. 'I'll get my change when I order,' he shouted to Sylvia, then removed his cold drink and began to gulp at the contents.

'Who's two haddock and chips?' Sylvia shouted above the sizzling and bubbling of yet another load of fish fresh into the fryer, and a cloud of steam enveloped her for a second or two, making her invisible.

'Over here! And I've got the right money,' called a voice from the other side of the counter, and an arm extended, hand clasping a pile of change, and the paper wrapped packet was given in exchange.

She had almost dealt with this deluge of customers, and there were only three people waiting to be served, when Frank Carrington strolled in. 'I thought I'd come in and give you a hand during the rush,' he announced, as if he were doing her a favour, rather than working in his own business to line his pocket, not hers.

'You know damned well we have a rush at ten, then another one just after eleven. Where were you at ten o'clock? I was in here getting broiled and working my guts out, just so as you can go on a nice holiday in the summer then swank about how well your business is doing.'

'Well, if you're not up to it anymore, Sylvia ...' he said, and left the sentence hanging.

'Don't you threaten me! You wouldn't get a fraction of the work out of a young 'un as you get out of me, and you know it. I'm more than value for money, and don't you forget it.'

'Only pulling your leg, Sylv. Don't get all hot and bothered about it.'

'Don't get all hot and bothered? Just look at the colour of my face, and my hair's dripping under this hat. You wouldn't know hot and bothered unless it had a sauna attached to it, you wouldn't.'

'Look, I'm here now, so let's not argue about it. The after-hours rush will be here any minute now, so make sure you've got enough chips ready, and plenty of batter. We can get on with some of the frying before they get here, so that at least we can serve the first dozen or so customers with what we pre-fry, then the next lot will be ready for the queue behind.'

'Makes sense to me. Get your coat and hat on then, and we'll get started for the first wave,' replied Sylvia, scooping the last of the chips out of the fat and adding a new batch.

The next wave arrived just a few minutes after eleven. and was the most difficult to deal with, because it consisted of those who had been in the pub just that little bit longer.

The queue was, unsurprisingly, not so well-behaved with the new batch of customers, and there was a fair amount of shoving and barging for position, and quite a few angry words exchanged as they waited.

Sylvia let fly. 'Get yourselves into a proper queue and act like civilised human beings. I don't care how much you've had to drink! If you want your chips from here, you can bloody well behave, or I'll chuck you out myself!'

She received some unexpected support from Frank Carrington, who raised his voice above the hubbub, and shouted, 'You'd better to listen to our Sylvia, because she means it, and I'm here to re-enforce her decisions.'

'Bloody little Hitler!' came from the middle of the queue, and Sylvia was on to it immediately. 'Dogger Ferguson, you get out of here this minute. I won't have talk like that in this chip shop, and you're barred.'

'You can't bar me! This is a chip shop, not a pub,' he replied, not really bothered by her threat.

'No, but *I* can!' This was Frank Carrington's voice, 'and *I'm* barring you. Get out now, and go quietly, or I'll call the police. I will not have insults like that bandied about in my chip shop. And if any of you think that's unfair, you can go too!'

'So where am I supposed to get my chips then,' the youth shouted back, now not looking so sure of himself.

'You'll just have to go into the town centre, won't you? Come back in six months, and I'll see if you've learnt any manners. Until then, don't come back!' This was from Sylvia, who was usually the one to restore order, if trouble seemed to be about to break out.

'Chalky White, you come back here this minute! Not only have you short-changed me, but one of the fifty pees is an old Irish one. You get back here, or I'll tell your mother!'

A dark-skinned youth wove his way back to the counter and corrected the transaction. 'God, I'm glad you're not my mother,' he said, as he left the counter.

'So am I!' called back Sylvia, giving as good as she got, 'Because if you were mine, I'd have drowned you at birth!'

'Old bitch!'

'I heard that!'

The rest of the evening was unusually aggressive, and by the time they had cleared up, prepped for the next day which, being Saturday, was a busy one, both she and Frank were exhausted.

'Where do they get it from? That's what I want to know,' said Sylvia, pulling on the old coat she always wore to work because she didn't want to smell like the lady from the chip shop wherever she went. This way, she didn't have to have any of her other coats sullied by the tell-tale smell of where she worked.

'The telly?' offered Frank. 'School?'

'More like the fact that their mums were only just out of school when they had 'em, and don't know a thing about bringing up a child to have good manners,' was Sylvia's considered opinion, and on this thought, Frank locked up. Sylvia got her bike out of the back hall and made her way home, another Friday evening over and done with. And good riddance to it, too, she thought, puffing and blowing her way back.

PORTION TWO

<u>Saturday 17th April – morning</u>

Detective Inspector Harry Falconer of the Market Darley CID was having a well-earned day off. Apart from other crimes, he had already dealt with three murder cases since his explosive entry to the New Year, courtesy of Carmichael's pantomime-themed wedding, and more booze than he'd ever indulged in in his life before, and that included his time in the army. He really needed a day away from the office and work, and had decided to indulge himself in one of his lazy days.

He'd not risen until half-past eight, a veritable lie-in for him, then treated himself to a fried breakfast, sharing the last rasher of bacon between his three cats, Mycroft, Tar Baby, and Ruby, who had all begged very nicely to share his unaccustomed treat.

After that, he'd spread the main body of his Saturday newspaper on the floor, laid down at the bottom of it, and begun to read. He was usually much more grown-up about this activity, but occasionally indulged in this sort of lounge on the floor because he enjoyed it, and holding up the paper (which was a broadsheet) made his arms ache, and, folding it, his temper ache.

He knew he wouldn't be able to stay in this position for long, because the cats so loved to play with the corners of the pages, stalking and pouncing on them, then chewing them a bit, and eventually, clawing them. He reckoned he had a good half an hour of shooing them off before he had to transfer the newspaper to the dining table. After that, he intended to watch an old black and white movie he had recorded weeks ago, and hadn't yet had the time to look at. And after that? Who knows? He might even go for a walk, or take a trip to the local garden centre.

In Castle Farthing, Detective Sergeant 'Davey' Carmichael was also enjoying a day off, and spending it with his wife, Kerry, and her two sons, Kyle and Dean. In his opinion, there was no better way to spend his leisure time than with these three dearest of people. They had also, recently, become the proud owners of two tiny dogs that the boys had named: a Chihuahua called Fang, and a miniature Yorkshire terrier called Mr Knuckles.

After an enormous breakfast – for, if Carmichael were a car, he'd be a gas guzzler, given his size and fuel consumption – he suggested that they all go out on to the village green and throw a stick and a ball around for the dogs. They had managed to find a very small ball in the pet shop that the young dogs could get their jaws round, and a twig sufficed, in their case, as a stick.

The boys were very enthusiastic, as were the dogs, for they loved getting out of the house and having a mad run around with the big man, and the green was so big to them. Kerry, however, pleaded household duties and, after closing the door on them gratefully, put on the washing machine, and sat down in her favourite armchair with a magazine and a cup of coffee. She already had a stew cooking away for their evening meal in the slow cooker, and felt that this was about as much as she wanted to do this morning.

Through the open window, it being such a fair day, she could hear the high-pitched yips of the dogs' excitement, and the voices of the boys calling after their pets. Occasionally her husband's voice boomed out with an instruction, but more often with laughter so, it seemed to her, that they were all having a jolly nice time, including herself in this thought.

Harry Falconer had finished with his newspaper for the time being, and was having a pre-luncheon doze on the sofa, covered in three furry bodies, joining him in this unexpected opportunity to use his body heat, when the phone rang. He started awake and sat up immediately, scattering cats as he got to his feet. This had better be a cold call. And if it was work, it'd better be good, disturbing him on the first day off he'd had for a fortnight.

'Falconer. What?' he answered, peremptorily.

'Harry, I'm so sorry to disturb you,' said the voice of Bob Bryant from the station, 'but there's been a very nasty death in Upper Darley. I think you need to get out there. And Carmichael.'

'What's happened? And why can't someone else handle it for a change?'

'I've spoken to Superintendent Chivers, and *he* wants you out there.'

'Sadistic bastard! Right! Where is it, and what happened?'

'It's at the chip shop on the Riverside Parade, in Upper Darley, and it's a nasty one. I don't even want to describe it. It turns my stomach.'

'And yet you want me to go out and *look* at it?'

'Sorry, Harry, but it is your job. Get yourself out there, and I'll send Carmichael to join you.'

'I'm on my way,' sighed Falconer. It was half-past twelve, and he now wouldn't have time for any lunch. And on his day off, too! Maybe he could snaffle a bag of chips when he got there.

The two little dogs, now exhausted, were having a nap on Kerry's lap when the phone rang in Jasmine Cottage, in Castle Farthing's High Street. Sliding them carefully off her, she rose to answer the phone. 'Hello, Bob,' she greeted the sergeant. 'Surely you're not going to disturb Davey on his day off? He hasn't had one for a couple of weeks, and he's out on the green, now, playing football with the boys.'

'Sorry, Mrs Carmichael. I wouldn't have called if the super hadn't insisted. Can you call him in, so that I can have a word?' asked Bryant, apologetically.

'Of course I can, and call me Kerry. Everyone else does. Hang on a moment,' she said, and put the receiver down on the little table where the phone base lived.

Opening the cottage door, she put her hands to her mouth, to create an improvised loud-hailer, and called, 'Davey – phone. Urgent!' and watched as he said a few words to the boys and sprinted back to the cottage, the boys trailing in his wake, evidently disappointed that their fun had been cut short on their day with Daddy Davey.

'Carmichael here,' said the sergeant, picking up the phone, wondering what could be so urgent on his day off.

'Davey, it's Bob from the station. There's been a nasty death at the chip shop, on that parade of shops at Upper Darley. Do you know the one? Good! The super wants you to meet Harry out there. You'll find out the details when you arrive.'

'But, what's hap ...' Carmichael started to ask, but Bob Bryant had cut him off, without a shred of detail. He'd just have to get himself over there as quickly as he could, and find out what had happened when he got there.

Falconer, living on the outskirts of Market Darley, was the first one to arrive on the scene, and found a crowd of would-be customers, now turned rubber-neckers, outside the plate glass window. Crime-scene tape had already been stretched across the front of the shop, and PC Merv Green was on duty at the door to keep sight-seers away, as far as was humanly possible. There was always an audience at the site of any public death. It was simple human nature, but not a nice side of it.

Pushing his way through the people gawking for a look through the window, he held out his warrant card and pushed his way through to where PC Green stood guard. 'Know what's happened in there?' he asked, before entering.

'Very nasty one, sir,' replied Green, his face in agreement with his name. 'I'm not usually squeamish, but this is a very unpleasant one. I think you'd better go inside and see for yourself. I don't want to think about it, let alone talk about it. Sorry, sir.'

This was unlike Green, and Bob Bryant had been reluctant to give any details either. Falconer's insides gave a little flip of apprehension as these two thoughts collided. These were both experienced policemen. Whatever could have given *them* such a fit of the heebie-jeebies? Wondering if Dr Christmas had already arrived, or was still on his way, he pushed open the glass door and went inside the chip shop, preparing for the worst.

'Hello, Harry,' said a familiar voice, and Falconer became aware of Dr Phillip Christmas and another man, standing at the back of the shop, well away from the fryers. 'May I introduce you to Frank Carrington, the owner of this establishment?'

Falconer approached and shook the man's hand, taking the opportunity to introduce himself at the same time. 'So, what have we got here?' he asked, and was surprised when the owner just pointed at the counter of the shop. After staring at this for a few seconds, Mr Carrington finally spoke, his voice a hoarse whisper. 'It's behind there!' he croaked. 'At the chip fryer.'

Christmas gave Falconer a look, and added, 'I hope you haven't already had your lunch, Harry. It's gruesome!'

'I haven't, as a matter of fact,' Falconer informed them, and then, finally reaching the other side of the counter, stopped dead, his mouth opening in surprise and horror, his eyes involuntarily closing to shut out what was in front of them.

Turning back to look at the other two men present, he opened his eyes again, and said, 'I think I might give lunch a miss today. Who the hell did this? It's iniquitous! What a bloody awful way to die!'

'Sorry, Harry. Wish I could have spared you this one,' sympathised Christmas. 'Maybe it'd be better if I told you what happened, rather than you poke around for yourself.'

'I think that's a very good idea. I don't fancy going any nearer to 'that' than I have to, and the thought of 'poking around', makes me positively queasy,' replied Falconer, joining them at the other end of the shop, well away from the fryers, where a couple of grotty tables and a few mismatched chairs were placed for anyone who wanted to dine-in.

'Take a seat, first, Harry. In fact, let's all sit down. It's not a nice subject for discussion, and I think we'd be better off seated once I start going into details.'

'Do I have to stay?' asked Carrington. 'After all, I found her, and I feel as sick as a dog.'

'Make a note of your name and address, and leave it on the counter, and I'll be in touch later,' Falconer told him, then waited until he'd complied before turning back to Dr Christmas. 'Come on, out with it. You know you've got to tell me sometime,' he said, looking apprehensive. 'Who? How? And when? And why, for God's sake. That's sick, and it took some doing. We'll work out who is responsible, when we've got something more to go on.'

Christmas drew a deep breath, and commenced his grisly tale. '"Who" is easy. The victim is a Mrs Sylvia Beeton, who had worked part-time here for years. I got her address from Mr Carrington, so you don't need to worry about that.

'"When' isn't too difficult, either, as she was supposed to arrive at work to get everything started at about eleven-thirty this morning, and open up at noon. Mr Carrington arrived just after opening time, and found customers waiting outside, unable to get in – she'd have locked the door while she did her preparation, and then not unlocked it again until opening time.

'That seems straightforward enough, so far,' Falconer interrupted the doctor, in a vain effort to delay what he knew would follow next.

'Oh, it is, but it's the 'how' that's the stomach-churner.' Here it came then. Falconer steeled himself for the grisly details. 'From what I could glean from an examination of the scene, when I arrived about fifteen minutes ago, someone dumped the large container of batter over her head, then pushed her head into the chip fryer, and held her down with the large chip scoop. As she was due to start pre-frying chips, the oil was up to temperature, and I'm afraid that's not very good for the complexion.'

'Oh, my good God!' exclaimed Falconer, unable to quite comprehend what he had been told. 'I'll have to take a look, for the sake of procedure, but now I know what happened, I know I'm not going to like it one little bit.'

Slowly, like a child who is afraid that someone might jump out at him, Falconer approached the other side of the counter, and moved towards the huge bulk of what, until nearly midday today, been Mrs Sylvia Beeton.

'Can you give me a hand to turn her over?' he called to Christmas. 'How did you manage it? She's a very big woman.'

'I got Green to help me,' explained the Doc, and followed Falconer behind the counter.

'That would explain why he looked so bilious when I got here,' replied Falconer, more as something to say to keep his mind off what he was about to see.

The two of them manhandled the body, so that they could look at its face, and Falconer came out in a cold sweat. 'Whoever it was, has literally fried her face, and in batter, too,' he managed, in a rather high-pitched voice, letting go his hold on his half of the mighty Mrs Beeton.

Christmas lowered his end too, and said, with a nervous little giggle, 'She's definitely been battered to death, then! And it looks like she was held down in there at the back of the neck, as I just said, with the chip scoop. I haven't touched it, just left it for you to put into an evidence bag, in case it's got fingerprints on it.'

'Don't joke about it, Philip. It only makes it worse. And I'll just get that scoop bagged up now. Thanks for noticing that. God, what a ghastly way to end up!'

'What a dreadful thing even to contemplate doing to another human being,' commented the medical man, and they both fell silent, and stared off into nothingness, horrified by this seemingly random and unspeakable act.

So deep were they in a brown study that they didn't hear the door open, and before either of them could do anything about it,

Carmichael sprung up like a jack-in-the-box beside them, full of enthusiasm, as usual, to see what was afoot; and, unfortunately, from this distance, he could do just that.

As he began to heave, Falconer yelled, 'Nooo!' and rushed, over in the vain hope that he could stem the inevitable flow. 'Footprints, man!' he shouted. 'Evidence!'

Hearing the inspector's voice, Carmichael swivelled his noxious spray a hundred and eighty degrees, and the last of his offering landed on the highly polished tops of Falconer's immaculate shoes.

'Now look what you've done, Sergeant! Muddied any forensic evidence on the floor. And just look at my shoes,' he finished, reaching for a roll of kitchen paper that sat on the shelf behind the counter. 'Why on earth didn't you wait?'

'Urgh!' groaned Carmichael, took a step forward to assist Falconer and slipped, landing on his back on his contribution to 'Dirty Floor Day.'

'And now you've fallen in it! Get yourself into the little cloakroom out the back, and see what you can do about cleaning yourself up!'

'You know I've got a dicky tummy, sir,' Carmichael pleaded, then, thinking again of what he had just seen, and went for it again with enthusiasm. But there was no ammunition left for him to shoot, and he stood there, in a pool of his own breakfast, dry-heaving like a pump fresh out of water.

'Sometimes I wonder why you joined the force!' snapped his boss, wiping lumps of the vile substance from his shoes, making a little moue of distaste, and making sure that he was breathing only through his mouth.

'Because I wanted to catch criminals, sir,' answered the sergeant, gingerly making his way towards the indicated cloakroom, and removing his jacket as he went.

'Well, that's ruined any evidence of footprints, this side of the counter!' said Falconer, a little later, looking daggers at his sergeant, who was perched on one of the old chairs at the back of the shop, his head between his knees. 'Why couldn't you have had a light breakfast for, once? Just look at the mess you've made of the crime scene!'

'Sorry, sir,' replied the ghost of Carmichael's voice. 'I couldn't help it. I'm surprised it didn't have the same effect on you, too.'

'Leave it, sergeant. I suppose *I'll* have to clear this away as best as I can before the SOCO team arrives, and I'd rather hoped to warn you to stay the other side of the counter before you came round here, but you just appeared out of nowhere, and it was too late by then.'

'What sort of evil person does that to someone?' Carmichael managed, his thought processes slowly re-gathering, his rinsed-off jacket in a chip shop plastic carrier bag at his feet. 'What sort of imagination could even think of doing something like that?'

'Don't ask me, Carmichael. Most people are all right, but a few of them, out there, are mad, bad, and dangerous to know, to coin a cliché. They're either just pure evil, or off their heads.'

'Hear, hear!' sounded, from where Philip Christmas was seated at another table, talking quietly into a recording device to aid his post mortem sometime later.

PORTION THREE

<u>Saturday 17th April – afternoon</u>

Neither Falconer nor Carmichael had been able to face any lunch, and when the SOCO team had arrived they left them to it and called into a coffee shop at the other end of the parade for a shot of caffeine.

'Oh, God, sir! I've never seen anything like that in my life before,' Carmichael almost breathed. 'All that bubbling! And her eyes! Bugger!' He suddenly went silent, and seemed to have a silent conversation with his innards, eventually adding, 'I think that's going to give me nightmares! Sorry about the language, sir.'

'Don't give it another thought, Carmichael. I think you've earned a bit of a swear after what you've witnessed this morning. Me, I think it was the batter that made it worse,' Falconer opined, in a low voice, so as not to alert too many people already in the coffee shop that they were police. 'And I agree with you. I think my sleep might be a bit disturbed for a few nights after this morning's little adventure.'

As Carmichael made a characteristic shrugging motion identical to the one he had made only a minute ago, Falconer looked at him in alarm, and hissed, 'And don't you dare be sick again. You can't have anything left after that magnificent demonstration back there!'

The sergeant sat as still as a statue for almost thirty seconds, his eyes closed, making a herculean effort to regain control of his internal muscles, then took a sip of coffee. 'So, where do we start, sir?' he asked. The spirit was willing, and the flesh recovering, at last.

'We ought to start with the owner, see if she made any enemies out of the customers. And I believe there are tenants in the upstairs flat. It might be worth having a word with them. Then we're going to have to have a look at where she lived: the usual stuff, although it was anything but a usual death, even for a murder.'

'While you were in that cloakroom, I got the address of the owner, and of Mrs Beeton, the – er – deceased. I think we should pay a little visit to Mr Carrington and ask if he remembers anything from last night that might have led to what we found this morning. There might also be regulars that she had fallen out with. He said she didn't mince her words, so that looks like our starting point, after the upstairs flat.'

'Mmph, sir.' Carmichael was still working on that internal control.

As the occupiers of the first floor flat above the chip shop were both office workers, they were at home, and not surprised to see the police after all the fuss that had been taking place downstairs since just before midday.

Before either of them could say anything, after the flat door had been opened, the young man who opened it asked, 'It's not about last night, is it? The music and everything?'

Falconer, not understanding what he was talking about merely echoed, 'Music?'

'We sometimes get a bit carried away on a Friday and Saturday night, and you can tell Mrs Beeton that we're really sorry. We'll think about other people in the future. We don't want to lose this flat, as we've only been here six months, and it's perfect for somewhere we can walk to work from.'

'Mrs Beeton asked you to turn your music down last night?' Falconer bluffed.

'Yeah! She was furious, because she had a rush on, and she couldn't hear the orders with us blaring out with the CD player. We're really sorry, and we'll apologise to her when we see her again. She was a bit of a dragon, though, which you'll know, if you've met her.'

'I'm afraid I haven't had that pleasure, sir. May I take your name, and that of your flatmate?'

'I'm Mark Manners, and my wife's name is Melanie,' he offered, and Falconer was surprised at the use of the term wife. The young man couldn't have been more than twenty-one or two.

'Well, Mr Manners, I'm afraid that Mrs Beeton was murdered a little before midday today, and I'm here to ask you whether you heard or saw anything about that time,' (and to see if her coming up here constantly to get you to turn your music down was enough to enrage you sufficiently to fry her face, he thought, but didn't vocalise).

Manners took a step backwards in surprise, and called over his shoulder, 'Mel, that chip shop woman has been murdered.'

There was a scuffling noise from the interior of the flat, and a young woman joined them, wearing only a dressing gown and slippers, yesterday's make-up a series of smears on her face, and her hair tousled and standing on end. 'What, that old moaning minnie who came up here last night? I don't believe it! Where did it happen? In the actual shop?'

'That's right, Mrs Manners. Just before midday.'

'I was asleep,' she stated baldly. 'Is that what you were trying to wake me up and tell me about, Mark?'

While they were speaking, Falconer had been thinking, and decided that, for now, they were wasting their time here. They could always call again and, if necessary, bring them down to the station for further questioning. If their noise nuisance had been persistent, and they were worried they might lose their tenancy, this might prove sufficient motive for doing away with the complainer.

After all, the owner probably wasn't on duty for the same number of hours that Sylvia Beeton was. What was the use of having a dog, and barking yourself? Maybe this very young couple had decided to take matters into their own hands before things came to a head, and Sylvia told the owner how often she had to go upstairs to tell them to turn the volume down. It was food for thought, at least.

Frank Carrington lived just a few streets away in Crescent Road, a pleasant curved development of detached 1930s houses, his being number nineteen. The garden was positively manicured, a car less than a year old stood on the drive, and pristine white net curtains showed at all the front windows.

'Very tidy!' commented Falconer, as they drew up at the kerb. 'Can't be too much of a hardship, serving fish and chips to the sort of rabble that buy them after chucking-out time, but I wouldn't fancy it on a Friday or Saturday night.'

'Me neither, but I wouldn't mind a couple of portions of his produce after work,' was Carmichael's reply, showing that he had obviously recovered from his unpleasant little outburst of Technicolor conceptual art.

'He did rather give the impression that he had employed Mrs Beeton for her strong personality, shall we say. Anyway, let's see what he can remember about who was in last night, shall we?'

Carrington answered the door almost before Falconer had taken his finger from the bell, and invited them into a house as immaculately kept as the garden. 'I'll just put the kettle on, then we can sit down with a cup of tea or coffee, and I'll tell you everything I know. I want whoever did this caught. Sylvia's been working part-time for me for as long as I can remember, and I want whoever did this locked away for a very long time.

'She started when her husband left her and she still had the kids at home, and when they left, she just carried on. Oh, but she was a good one with handling trouble. I've seen her pick some troublesome lad up by the scruff of the neck and hurl him out of the door without batting an eyelid. I won't be a minute. Go in and make yourselves comfortable,' he concluded, disappearing off into what they could see was the kitchen, another room that sparkled with loving buffing and cleaning.

The two detectives went through a door that evidently led to the sitting room, and found it furnished with plush leather furniture at one end, and an antique dining table and chairs at the other. Settling, each of them, into an armchair, and almost disappearing into its feather-filled cushions, they waited in silence until Carrington returned, a large tray in his hands.

'I didn't ask you what you wanted, but I thought tea would be all right? I can make coffee if you prefer, though,' he declared, setting down the tray on a marble coffee table.

'Tea's fine,' confirmed Carmichael.

'Just the ticket,' agreed Falconer, and Carrington began to dispense the fragrant liquid.

'Milk? Yes? Right. Help yourselves to sugar,' he suggested, as he handed them their cups, then stared on in disbelief as Carmichael added six spoonfuls of sugar to his cup, nearly emptying the little sugar bowl.

'Don't worry about me,' Falconer hastily stated. 'I don't take sugar,' as if this would be consolation enough to their host. He was used by now to Carmichael's preference for sticky tea that could almost, but not quite, be sliced.

'Me neither,' muttered Carrington. 'Now,' at a more normal volume, 'How can I be of assistance? I've made a note of anyone I saw or heard misbehaving yesterday evening, and of any Sylvia mentioned when we were chatting, clearing up. It's the usual suspects, I'm afraid, and she actually had to take the unusual step of barring one of them, 'Dogger' Ferguson, last night. I don't think I've known her ever do that before, but I don't know whether I can back that up, now she's gone.'

So, Sylvia Beeton had been employed to be the chip shop 'heavy', and Mr Carrington was one of those weak men whom he would like to advise to 'grow a backbone'. Hiding behind the stronger personality of a woman was despicable, in his opinion.

Suddenly, Carrington looked woebegone and lost, and Falconer realised how much he would miss the woman, if she had worked for him for as long as he said she had. 'Let's have those names then, sir,' he requested, and Carmichael extracted his notebook, after having made short work of the plate of biscuits that had also sat on the tray, and was now sadly decorated with only a few crumbs.

Noticing this for the first time, Falconer exclaimed, 'Carmichael! You've eaten *all* the biscuits!'

'Oh, sorry Mr Carrington, but I lost my breakfast,' he shuddered as he remembered, 'and I didn't feel like any lunch.'

'Don't worry, Sergeant. A few biscuits isn't going to bankrupt me. I've got a little list here: 'Spike' Ellis, 'Dogger' Ferguson, 'Troll' Norman, 'Darkie' Collins, 'Chalky' White, and 'Curry' Khan. They were the main offenders. I've known them all since their mums used to bring them along in their prams and pushchairs to get a bag of chips for their tea.

'And nice kids they were, too, but you know what happens to them these days, once they get to a certain age. Once the acne gets them, they discover fags, booze, joints, and girls, and suddenly they're all like Jekyll and Hyde, especially on Friday and Saturday nights. They've got really mouthy over the last year or so.'

'But Mrs Beeton kept them in line, did she?' asked Falconer.

'As best she could, but they were getting worse. She wouldn't stand for any nonsense when she was serving, and she gave as good as she got. Her father was a sailor, and, boy, could he cuss! She learnt well from him.'

'Anyone else you can think of who might bear her a grudge?' was his final question.

'No one. She was a fine specimen of her kind, and she'll be sorely missed in the shop.'

Back in the car, Falconer turned a suddenly optimistic face to Carmichael, and said, 'I recognise most of those names. They've all been in trouble at some time or other over the last eighteen months or so, so we'll have no problem with their addresses, and the ones not known to the police will be easy to find, because we'll make sure we get their addresses from the others.'

'That'll save a lot of time. We can just look them up on the computer, and we'll be able to go there knowing what they've already been up to.'

'Just so! Forewarned is forearmed!'

PORTION FOUR

<u>Saturday 17th April, – later</u>

Back at the station, they looked up the records of the names of the four youths that both of them were familiar with, and it was the usual story of the times, for between them they had been brought in for: taking a motor vehicle without the owner's consent, being drunk and disorderly, breach of the peace, brawling, possession of cannabis, and a bit of shop-lifting, just to add spice to the mix.

Dogger Ferguson had narrowly missed being prosecuted for assaulting a police officer, but as the officer was PC Merv Green, who was soft-hearted underneath his gruff exterior, he had not pressed charges, and the incident merely remained on file.

The two names currently unknown to the police were Darkie Collins and Curry Khan, but Falconer had every confidence that they would pick up their addresses from their mates. The other four all lived on an estate consisting mostly of blocks of flats; not high-rises – only four floors – but even these were a blot on the Market Darley/ Upper Darley landscape, and a source of much of the trouble caused by teenagers and tearaways in the town and in the surrounding area.

Their first call was to the home of Spike Ellis, seventeen years old, and with three convictions for shoplifting to his name. The flat was in Robin House, as this was the Wild Birds Estate, and on the top floor, the lift, or course, being out of order. The entrance hall smelt of vomit and urine, and Carmichael clapped his handkerchief to his mouth and nose as soon as they entered.

'Don't touch the bannister rail,' warned Falconer, who had been caught like this before. Some clever individuals, in their cups, found it hilarious to smear bannister rails with faeces, and others, of a more pathological bent, liked to embed bits of broken glass in them, or even razor blades.

The top landing had four doors, all desperately in need of a coat of paint and, from the door with the number sixteen on it, (in drunken brass numerals, their original quota of fixing screws now reduced to one each) blared loud music, the sound of a baby yelling, and a female voice shouting abuse at one of the other occupants.

Falconer left it for Carmichael to use his mighty fist to knock, and when that produced no reaction from within, shouted himself, 'Open up. Police!'

There was a sudden silence within, with the exception of the wails of the baby, and a woman with dyed blonde hair, her roots almost half its length, and last night's heavy make-up making an artist's palette of her face, opened the door and grunted, 'Wotcher want? My Spike ain't done nuffink! Whenever it was, 'e was 'ere wiv me. Gottit?'

'Good morning Mrs Ellis,' Falconer opened for his side, and immediately had the legs cut from under him.

'That's *Miss* Ellis. Spike's old man did a runner when 'e found out I was up the duff, and I ain't seen 'im since, if yer must know.'

Falconer tried again. 'Good morning *Miss* Ellis. I wonder if we could have a word with your son – er – Spike, if it's not too much trouble. It won't take a minute, if we could just step inside.'

Miss Ellis turned, and bellowed, 'Spike, you get your arse out 'ere this minute. Wot you been up to now, yer little bastard?'

As they entered the flat, Carmichael wishing he could use his handkerchief here, too, a spindly, spotty youth with his hair dyed orange came out of one of the doors and stared at the visitors, perplexed.

Falconer took a moment to adjust to the smell and, surreptitiously looking round what he could see of the flat, took in overflowing ashtrays, empty beer and lager cans, and at least three rolled-up and very used disposable nappies just lying on the floor, un-regarded. The curtains were still drawn, there were newspapers and baby toys scattered across the floor and the furniture, and a collection of mugs and plates, unwashed and discarded after use.

''E's only seventeen. You've gotta 'ave me present, cos I'm what they call an appropriate adult,' Miss Ellis informed them, picking up the baby and lighting a cigarette at the same time.

How well their social workers taught them these days, thought Falconer, before turning his full attention to Spike, who looked very wary now, and beat him to it, by announcing, 'I ain't done nuffink! You can't pin anyfink on me, cos I ain't done nuffink.'

'I only want to know where you were first thing this morning, Spike, and to confirm where you were yesterday evening.'

'D'yer wanna sit down?' interrupted Miss Ellis, intent on being as much of a nuisance as she could. She might have been yelling her head off at Spike just a few minutes before, but he was her baby, and she would protect him fiercely to the end.

'No, thank you,' squeaked Carmichael, determined not to draw a deep breath in this flat.

'Spike?' Falconer encouraged the youth.

'I've only just woke up,' Spike mumbled. 'That's what me mum was yellin' about when you come knockin' on the door just now.'

''E's a real lazy little sod sometimes,' added his mother, as an aside, then added, ''e didn't come in till Gawd knows what time last night, then 'e can't get up in the mornin'. Just like 'is dad, 'e'll turn out. Never 'old down a job, nor nuffink like that. Waste o' space, 'e is at the moment.'

'I'd rather you didn't interrupt during questioning, if you don't mind, Miss Ellis. It's Spike I would like to give me information,' said Falconer, his temper rising.

'Sorry for breavin',' Spike's mother snapped back at him, and sat down in a filthy, food-stained armchair and stubbed out her cigarette on a ketchup-stained plate.

'Where did you get up to yesterday evening, Spike?' Falconer asked, mentally keeping his fingers crossed that the youth's mother would butt out of the conversation and let him get on with his job in peace.

'Not a lot,' Spike answered. 'We got Dogger to blag some extra-strong cider from the 'offie', and some real head-bangin' lagers. We drunk a few, then went round the old car ports and smoked a joint or two' – this young man knew about the changes in the law that no longer made smoking a little cannabis a prosecutable offence – 'then o' course, we got the munchies, so we stashed the booze, and went down the chippie on the parade.

'After that, we went back to the car ports, and finished off the booze. I was wasted when I got in, and I've just woke up, like I told yer.'

'And who was with you?'

'Dogger, like I said, Troll, Chalky, Darkie, and old Curry. That's us. The cool dudes!'

'So, let me get this straight. You got one of your friends to buy alcohol from the off-licence, for under-age drinkers, then you smoked some drugs, then went to the chip shop, came back to the estate, and continued to drink until you came home.'

'That's it. Wot else d'yer wanna know?'

'Did you wake up earlier than just now, and go to the parade to visit the chip shop again, possibly because of something that happened when you were there yesterday evening?'

'Shit! I told yer. I dinn't wake up till just now. 'Ow could I 'ave gone out, when I never woke up?'

'Thank you very much. We'll be on our way, then. Goodbye.'

'So much for family life in the enlightened twenty-first century,' Falconer commented to Carmichael as they finally reached the blessed fresh air again, and headed for the car.

'How can they live like that?' asked Carmichael. 'No wonder we have so much trouble with the kids today, if they come from places like that. And she's got a baby. Imagine having to get a pram or pushchair up and down all those stairs, when the lifts are out of order!'

'Which is always,' said Falconer, concluding the conversation.

Four more of the names they had been given came from similar blocks on the same estate, and the interviews began with either a youth only just risen, or, in two cases, not even out of bed yet, and the day was getting on. Their trail led them variously to Blackbird House, Starling House, Goldfinch House, and Jackdaw House, and each block was as depressing as the first had been.

The only positive information that they received were the addresses of Darkie Collins and Curry Khan, neither of whom lived on the Wild Birds, and which they decided to visit after they had had a look at Sylvia Beeton's house and spoken to her neighbours.

They had obtained the keys of her house from her handbag at the chip shop, and set off now for Meadow Road which, now that they thought about it, wasn't too far from Crescent Road, so they should, logically, have gone there first, before taking themselves off to the Wild Birds Estate.

Meadow Road was a little less up-market than Crescent Road, but was comprised of tidy pairs of thirties semis. Sylvia's was a left-handed one, as one looked at the pair, and was in stark contrast to the condition of its mirror twin.

In fact, the gardens all along that side of the road were well-kept, with flower beds, displays of roses and shrubs, and lawns green and rich. Sylvia's was the exception. The beds that existed had only shrubs in them, although they were not overgrown and neglected, and the lawn, though neatly trimmed, was more weeds and moss than grass. It was perfectly tidy; just not planted and pandered to with the obsessiveness evident in the neighbouring gardens.

To the right of the boundary with the right-hand semi rose a veritable Everest of Leylandii hedging, beautifully trimmed right up to the edge of the path next door, but sprawling right over the path leading to the door of Sylvia's house, and even infringing on the lawn in the middle of its length.

'Definitely not an avid gardener, then, like her neighbours,' commented Falconer, picking his way to the door. 'More 'just keeping it tidy', like the average mortal.'

'Surprised she could get her bike up the path,' added Carmichael, thinking of the bicycle that still resided in the area at the back of the chip shop.

'You can see the tracks of her tyres on the lawn from where it was wet earlier in the week,' Falconer pointed out, removing her door key from his pocket and opening the door. 'I don't know what we expect to find in here, but we'd better have a look around, in case she had any threatening letters or anything like that.'

'Wouldn't she have confided in Mr Carrington?' asked Carmichael. 'They'd worked together for years.'

'You're probably right, but let's just take a quick look round, then we can pay a call on the neighbours and find out what they have to say about her.'

The inside of the property was in much better order than the garden, and it appeared that Sylvia Beeton had led a clean and tidy life behind closed doors. Even the cup and bowl that she had presumably used for her breakfast this morning were standing, rinsed, and upside down on the draining board, the dish-cloth hung over the mixer tap to dry.

After less than half an hour of poking and prying, Falconer called it a day. 'Come on, Carmichael,' he said, summoning the sergeant from working his way through the sideboard. 'We'll go next door and find out what sort of a neighbour she was.'

A cold welcome awaited them at the property to the right of Sylvia's house; the one with the regimented garden that looked like it had had its lawn trimmed with a manicure set. Its owner, David Mortimer, was a man who appeared to be in his mid-fifties, his grey hair close-trimmed, rather like his grass. He had a small toothbrush moustache and wore a cardigan and slippers, highlighting, thought Falconer, the fact that this was a Saturday and, for him, at least, a day of leisure.

'I'm calling about your neighbour, Mrs Sylvia Beeton. I don't know whether it's been on local radio yet ...?' Falconer began his questioning, after introductions had been carried out.

'It has, but I really have no opinion on the matter,' replied Mortimer, his eyes cold and disinterested.

'We just wanted to get an idea of what she was like as a neighbour – you know the sort of thing. Had she fallen out with anybody, to your knowledge? Had there been any trouble at the house, recently?'

'I keep myself to myself, Inspector. I do not waste time gossiping with the neighbours, and have no interest whatsoever in the ins and outs of their private lives. I'm afraid I can't help you at all,' he announced, and swiftly closed the door in their faces.

'What a miserable old sod,' said Falconer. 'People aren't usually that unhelpful.'

At the house to the left of Sylvia's, the occupant introduced herself as Mrs Hare (but call me Maude, everybody else does), who patted at her hair in a coquettish way as she spoke to them, even though she proved to be a widow, and was in her early eighties.

'And what can I do for you two young gentlemen?' she asked them, smoothing down the wrinkles in her skirt.

'We're here about your neighbour, Sylvia Beeton,' Falconer informed her.

'What? You'll have to speak up, young man. I don't hear as well as I used to.'

'SYLVIA BEETON,' Falconer repeated.

'Oh, you'll be asking about that hedge at her property,' said Mrs Hare, with a knowing nod of her head. 'Well, I don't get involved with anything of that sort.'

'NO!' roared Falconer, SHE'S DEAD!'

'She's done what, dearie?' asked the elderly woman, cupping a hand to an ear and leaning forward.

'SHE'S BEEN MURDERED!' shouted Falconer.

'Oh, that's nice for her. I hope she enjoys herself. Well, I mustn't stand here on the doorstep gossiping and letting the heat out. Thank you for telling me, young man,' and with that, Mrs Hare closed the door with a smile, and just the hint of a twinkle in her faded old eyes.

'Bloody marvellous!' exclaimed Falconer. 'We come out here to find out about the woman's character, and one neighbour lives like a recluse, and the other's as deaf as a post. Let's get off to those other two addresses, and call it a day for today.'

PORTION FIVE

<u>Saturday 17th April – even later</u>

Darkie Collins lived in Jubilee Terrace, a string of houses dating from the turn of the twentieth century, and obviously built to celebrate Queen Victoria's Diamond Jubilee. Forming the other side of the street was Victoria Terrace, dating from the same era. The front gardens were minimal, consisting of only a few feet of land between the boundary and the house, but this area of number thirteen was full of spring flowers in pots and tubs.

The woman who opened the door was very dark skinned, and had one of the widest smiles Falconer had ever seen. How could anyone get so many teeth into one mouth? he thought, as she beamed a welcome at them. 'Mrs Collins?' he enquired, hopefully, and she immediately corrected him,

'Miss Collins. I haven't yet persuaded a good man to put a ring on my finger,' she informed him, and smiled again, as if this was one of the most amusing things she had ever said.

'Miss Collins. I'm here to speak to your son, if he's at home. Is that possible?'

'Winston? What's he done?' she asked, and turned her head back inside the narrow hall and yelled, 'Winston, you get yo' ass down here. Now!' then turned her hundred watt smile back round to the two detectives and said, as sweetly as they could have wished, 'Would you like to come inside for a cup of tea?'

She showed them into a tiny sitting room, where the chairs and sofa were covered with bright throws, and vividly-coloured abstract paintings hung from the walls. As she disappeared off to the kitchen, a clattering down the stairs announced the arrival of Winston, and he came straight in to see what was happening.

Winston proved to be much lighter-skinned than his mother, but his complexion confirmed why his friends called him Darkie. When asked why he tolerated this, his reply was pragmatic. 'Well, it's better than "nigger", which was what they called me before they got to know me. And you've got to be part of the hard crew, or you get beaten up. It's self-protection, innit, mate?'

His mother reappeared carrying a tin tray with four mugs on it. 'I made one for you, too, Winston,' she informed her son, then continued, 'What you been up to, boy? You in trouble?'

'I just want to know where your son was this morning, Miss Collins,' Falconer informed her.

'He's old enough to speak for himself now,' she said, looking at her son as he lounged in a chair. 'And sit up straight when we've got visitors.'

Winston hauled himself into a vaguely upright position, and replied to Falconer's query. 'I've been upstairs all morning doing my homework.' His accent had definitely lost that twang of Jamaican that it had had when he had first spoken.

'Did you know Mrs Beeton, who served in the chip shop, on the parade?'

'Sure I know her. I've known her since I was a little tiny kid. She shouts loud, but she don't mean nothin' by it.'

'Did you see her last night?' Falconer was approaching the nub of the matter.

'Sure I saw her last night. Me and my mates went there for some chips, and to hang out and chill,' he replied, without any hint that he knew what had happened.

'Did you and your mates fall out with her?'

'Sure, we had words, but dat's de game, innit? It don't mean a ting, man. Jost de banter and stoff.'

'Winston, don't you use that silly accent under my roof. I've told you before, you've been brought up properly, so you speak properly too.'

'Sorry, Ma,' he apologised, then disarmed his mother with a huge grin. 'Gotcha!'

Interrupting this tender parent/child moment, Falconer asked, 'Did you know she was dead, Winston?'

'No way!' he shouted.

'She can't be,' exclaimed his mother. 'Was it an accident, or a heart attack, or something like that. She was one big woman.'

'I'm sorry to have to tell you that she was murdered, late this morning.'

There was a silence that threatened to cause a real hiatus in the interview, until Falconer gave it a little nudge by asking, 'Did you, by any chance, slip down to the parade this morning, Winston?'

Two voices angrily assured both policemen that the boy hadn't left his room, except for two cups of coffee and a bathroom break.

'Did any of your friends have a particular grudge against her, for something she'd said or done?' he continued.

'Nuh! But Dogger Ferguson did say more than once that she needed a good slap, like all women.'

'Winston!'

'Well, he did! He's an animal, and always saying things like that, but he doesn't mean anything by it.'

Three heavy sighs followed this casual reference to violence and women, and this time it was Miss Collins who broke it. 'It's that estate!' she said, obviously referring to the Wild Birds. 'We used to live there too, when I was left on my own with Winston, but I scrimped and saved to do an Open University degree, and then trained as a social worker so that we could have a better life.

'I bought this house for a song, seeing as it was number thirteen, and so many people have silly superstitious natures. We moved here three years ago, but Winston still hangs around with the old crowd from the blocks.

'I can't believe old Sylvie's dead, though. She's been serving me since Winston was in his pushchair.'

'Mum!'

'And you're absolutely certain that Winston never set foot outside this house this morning, Mrs Collins?'

'I would swear it on the Bible, Inspector.'

'And you can't think of anything that happened, that might have triggered off a fit of rage in one of your friends, Winston?'

'No, man! Not even Dogger would waste anyone!'

Curry Khan lived in a large modern detached house in the fairly new development: King's Acre. There was a Mercedes parked on one side of the double drive, a BMW on the other, and an elderly man working away in the garden, clearing away dead growth so that the spring flowers could grow uninhibited.

'Very nice,' was Falconer's comment, as they parked.

'Too flash!' was Carmichael's simultaneous opinion.

The door was opened by a tiny woman in a sari, who immediately went to fetch a man they presumed was their husband. 'Mr Khan?' enquired Falconer, holding out his hand in greeting.

His assumption was correct, and soon they were all four seated in the large sitting room at the back of the house, from which a fair-sized conservatory opened out.

'I wonder if I could speak to your son, Mr Khan. I'm afraid I don't know his real Chr ... hrmph! His forename, as we've only ever heard him referred to by his, um, nickname.' Falconer had nearly put his foot right in it, by referring to the man's son's Christian name. Life was so much more complicated these days!

'What? Curry?' asked Mr Khan, his face beaming at them, as he said this. 'They might call him that because of his ethnic origins, but if they knew how much I make from my Indian restaurants – I've got three, you know – they might use it as a term of respect, for he will have a very good inheritance.'

'How lovely!' Falconer congratulated him, not quite knowing how to respond to a reference to circumstances under which his current host would be dead. 'Is it possible for us to have a word with him?'

'Of course, Inspector. He is in his study, doing his schoolwork. Indira will fetch him for you.' The tiny woman left the room on this errand, returning shortly with a slim and elegant young man who introduced himself as Sanjeev, and took a seat looking expectantly at the two visitors.

'Good afternoon,' Falconer greeted him formally. It seemed like that sort of household, to him. 'I wonder if you could tell me where you have been this morning – all of it,' he added, in case the lad had slipped out before attending to his homework.

'I had a shower and ate my breakfast,' Sanjeev began, talking the question literally, 'Then, I went to my study to attend to my homework. When I had finished that, my mother brought me a cup of tea, and I did some research on the internet. I was still engaged in that activity when you rang the doorbell,' he explained, precisely and succinctly.

'You didn't leave the house at all?'

'Not even for one minute, I assure you.'

'What does this questioning concern, Inspector? I would like to know why you are visiting my house today,' asked Sanjeev's father.

'A woman who worked at the chip shop on the parade has, most unfortunately, been found dead this morning, and we are of the opinion that she was murdered, and that your son was in the chip shop last night.'

'No! Sanjeev?' shouted Mr Khan, rising from his seat.

'I'm so sorry, Papa! I'm so sorry!'

The boy's face was crumpled in anguish, and anger suffused his father's expression, his face red and his fists clenched.

Falconer's eyes widened at what was unfolding in front of him, and Carmichael was so startled in the change of atmosphere that he dropped his pencil, and had to grovel around under the wooden dining chair on which he was sitting to find it again.

The inspector began to rise from his seat, steeling himself to administer a caution before arrest, when Mr Khan spoke again. 'So, you have been buying chips again; when I have three restaurants from which you could get free food whenever you wanted it. My *son*! *My* son, buying chips! Oh, the shame of it!'

'I am so sorry, Papa. It was only because I was with my friends. I won't go in there again. I promise. I promise you, on my word of honour, Papa!'

Falconer sank back into his chair again, and gave a small cough of embarrassment. 'I think I have all the information I need from your son, and we'll take our leave of you now. Don't worry: we can see ourselves out,' he squeaked, and he and Carmichael fairly scarpered back to the car.

Once back behind the wheel, Carmichael gave Falconer a long stare of bewilderment, and the inspector turned to him and said, 'There are some cultural gaps too wide to cross, Carmichael.'

Back at the station, Falconer asked his sergeant to go through his notes to see if there was anything in there to give them a pointer. The four interviews he had conducted on the Wild Birds Estate had left his head in a whirl, with all the shouting, the bad language, and the squalor and he could remember little of what was actually said.

'Well, nobody actually owned up to anything, and I don't have a lot of notes, because I left out all the swear words.'

'There are decent people living in those blocks, Carmichael. It just happens that the ones we spoke to today are particularly, um, deprived,' Falconer stated, being absolutely fair. This morning visits only represented a minority of the flats' tenants.

'None of them liked her that much. They all thought she was loud and mouthy. And bossy, too. And that couple who lived over the shop weren't too keen, either.'

'She had to be, working in a place like that. I expect that was why Mr Carrington has kept her on for so long. He needs, or needed, someone who could not only serve and give change, but could act as a bouncer as well. It would seem that Sylvia Beeton fulfilled all these criteria.'

At that moment, the telephone rang, and Falconer grabbed at the receiver. 'Inspector Falconer: Market Darley CID. How may I help you? Oh, Philip it's you. If I'd known it was you, I'd have blown my whistle down the phone and hung up.'

'Ha ha! Very funny! You're only sulking because of what happened to your shoes at the locus. You can't fool me, Harry, old boy,' replied the doctor.

'What can I do for you?'

'I just felt I had to phone you, to say that I've never had a body before that I didn't know whether to douse in salt and vinegar or examine. I shall dine out on this story for months, thanks to you.'

'Philip?'

'Yes, Harry?'

'Go away, before I commit another murder in the area; one that you won't be able to be around to deal with,' he threatened, and hung up.

'What did the doc want?' asked Carmichael.

'Nothing. It wasn't important.' If he'd told Carmichael what Philip Christmas had just said, there was no telling how the sergeant would react, and he'd only just got his shoes clean again. 'Have we got anything at all?'

I don't think so, sir. It must have been some passing nutter, I suppose.'

'I don't buy that, Carmichael. There's more to this than meets the eye, and I'm going to get to the bottom of it, if it's the last thing I do.'

PORTION SIX

<u>Monday 18th April</u>

Over the weekend, Falconer had had a recurring dream: one that forced him to revisit Sylvia Beeton's house and stare at it long and hard. There was something tickling at the back of his mind, and he needed it to jump forward and declare itself. The answer was within his grasp: he just hadn't recognised it yet.

Monday morning found him in the office very early, making a list of telephone numbers, which he worked his way through shortly after arriving at the station, hoping to catch people before they left for work.

He hit pay dirt on his fourth call, then made another call, to round off his activities for the morning, being passed from department to department until he found what he was after. After a few minutes' reflection, he dialled again, to ascertain that he would be able to carry out what he wanted to do, then sat twiddling his thumbs until Carmichael arrived, too excited to settle to do anything, yet exasperated at how slowly time was crawling by. The sergeant wasn't due on duty until nine thirty this morning, and Falconer snorted his disgust and chagrin that the man had not been rostered for an earlier shift.

The hands of the clock slowly ground their way round to five, four, three, two minutes to the half hour, then the door of the office burst open, and a bright and sunny figure lolloped into the room, shedding its jacket as it went. 'Morning, sir. Anything happening?' it asked.

The tension suddenly left Falconer's body now that his partner was there, and he slumped in his chair. 'Yes, Carmichael. I've solved the case!'

You've done what?'

'I know who killed Mrs Beeton from the chip shop!'

'You what?'

'I know who did it, Carmichael. Am I speaking Swahili or something today, or are you just incapable of understanding me anymore?'

'Sorry, sir,' said Carmichael, sitting down.

'Now, you listen up, my lad, and listen good. I'm going to tell you a little story – but not all of it, yet – then we're going out to make an arrest,' Falconer declared, and proceeded so to do.

David Mortimer submitted, without fuss, to being arrested, merely taking one more look at his immaculate garden as he was led away, and pausing to spit over the garden gate at his next door neighbour Sylvia Beeton's house. There had been no resistance at all, and he had readily admitted what he had done in a fit of rage and depression.

'So it was as simple as that, was it?' asked Carmichael, after Mortimer had been taken away in a squad car, and they were driving back to the station.

'We got nothing from those boys, no matter how intimidating their behaviour might have been, when they're out in public, and I couldn't see any signs of guilt from any one of them. The only thing that stuck in my mind was what that deaf old lady – what was her name? Maude Hare, I think – said when we arrived.

'She thought we'd come about a hedge. I thought she was just rambling, because of her age and lack of hearing, but I did notice that she had a neat little privet hedge, and Mrs Beeton had a fence, so I just dismissed what she'd said. And then, both nights at the weekend, I dreamt I was being consumed by a giant hedge, and I couldn't find any way out of it. It wasn't like a maze, you understand: just a huge hedge.

'Well, then I remembered that, at Mrs Beeton's house, the hedge between her property and the one on the right was a huge monstrosity of Leylandii, and that her side of it grew right across the pathway, but on the other side, it was carefully trimmed and kept in shape.

'Did Mrs Hare think we were from the Council, I wondered, and today, after I'd made a few other calls, I phoned up the local authority, and got myself on a real merry-go-round of extensions, until I found out that a complaint had been lodged some time ago.

'I'd already phoned the tree surgeons I was able to find in the Yellow Pages, and, on the fourth call, I found one who had an appointment to go to Mrs Beeton's house this week and cut down a hedge of Leylandii. The council had told me there was nothing they could do for the woman, and advised her to go to the Citizens Advice Bureau. It wasn't her hedge you see.

'They'd told her she could trim the offending branches, and even put the cuttings on to her neighbour's land, to prove that she hadn't stolen his property, but she wanted to find a way to get rid of the hedge altogether, because it blocked so much light from the front of her house, and it looks like she was willing to pay to get the job done without permission.

'A further search of her house produced a file of letters between their solicitors about removing the light-blocking eyesore. They were in that sideboard I called you away from, when I mistakenly thought there was nothing there for us. The situation had come to an impasse, however, and another visit to Mrs Hare, with the word 'hedge' shouted very loudly, produced the information that they – Mrs Beeton and Mr Mortimer – were frequently going hammer-and-tongs at it about the hedge, out on the street.

'Mortimer said – you heard him yourself – that she told him this morning that she was 'going to have the bloody things cut down and burnt', and she'd like to see him stop her. He spent a couple of hours working himself into a real rage and downing shots of scotch, then went round to the chip shop and confronted her, and that was that. What a waste of both lives! And the fool had left his fingerprints all over the chip scoop, so there was no chance of him bluffing his way out of it.'

They were just passing the end of the pedestrian High Street, when Carmichael suddenly yelled, 'Stop!'

Falconer did a fairly good impression of an emergency stop, and looked at his partner quizzically. Whatever is it, Sergeant? What's the matter?'

'I just fancied a bag of chips, and there's a chip shop on that corner back there. I might even have a battered burger with it.'

'Well, it has been at least two hours since your breakfast,' replied Falconer, then leaned out of the car window and shouted, 'Could you get the same for me as well; and lots of vinegar, Carmichael.'

THE END

Toxic Gossip

DI Falconer becomes involved in a gossip-fuelled hate crime, only to find himself questioning his own judgement when it comes to protecting Miriam Darling from her anonymous persecutors...

Chapter One

Friday 6th August

Miriam Darling stood in her new sitting room, missing suddenly the hurly-burly of the removal men and their cheery banter as they had transferred all her worldly goods into her new home.

Since yesterday afternoon, her world had been filled with these energetic and talkative men. First, as they packed her precious breakables, and loaded most of her furniture into their large van, leaving her only a bed and the means of making them all a cup of tea in the morning, and again today, as they moved her two hundred miles to her new address.

At first, she had found their inconsequential chatter a nuisance, and had taken herself off to the garden to sit on an old stool on the patio, but, as the afternoon wore on, she had found herself going indoors more frequently, coming, little by little, to enjoy the sound of life in the home that she would be leaving the next day, forever.

By mid-afternoon, she found herself in the kitchen, brewing a pot of tea, and scrabbling round in her almost bare cupboards for a packet of biscuits. Sugar for energy, she thought, as her searching hand fell upon a packet of chocolate digestives she didn't realise she still had.

A tea-break meant a sit-down, and they settled themselves happily on the sitting room floor, now bare of its furniture and all its decorative trappings and pictures. She was just about to leave them to enjoy their tea and biscuits in peace when one of them called to her to join them if she wanted to, and, quite unexpectedly, she found that she did want to sit down with them, and engage in a normal conversation, for the first time in months.

They really were a jolly crew, who clearly enjoyed their work and their travels, and got on well with each other. As she sipped at her hot drink and nibbled on a biscuit, they regaled her with tales from their various trips together, exaggerating the mishaps and disasters to such an extent that she found herself laughing, and was grateful for their happy banter.

When they finished for the evening and took a taxi to a local public house to eat their evening meal, she threw the last of her left-over food together for a make-shift meal and contemplated the fact that, after today, this house would no longer be her home. That a new start was a good idea, she had no doubt, but she had lived at the same address for so long that not having the address any more would feel like an amputation – a new telephone number in her head, like a betrayal of who she was and how she had got to be this woman called Miriam Darling.

A new area would allow her to become someone new – someone whom nobody pitied and no one sought to comfort, or pointed out in the street, whispering to their companion about her history. Somewhere else, she would just be 'that woman who'd just moved into the house on the corner'. She could be anonymous, and start life afresh, with a clean sheet, provided she could banish the memories and, somehow, suppress the nightmares.

Today had started in a whirl of activity, making sure that the old house was in a fit and presentable state to greet its new owners, and that nothing had been forgotten. At the last minute, she had grabbed the old kitchen clock from the wall, where it had been abandoned for no good reason, and carried it out to her car, to put it safely on the back seat where it would not be jostled around too much.

And then they were off, at six o'clock on a Friday morning, heading for pastures new; leaving everything familiar and previously comforting behind. Following the removal van, she let her mind wander as she kept the vehicle in easy sight, due to its sheer bulk. She tried to remember all she could of the town and street she had chosen for the next phase of her life, and the few people she had met so far in her visits to the new address.

These, given the distance between the two places and the infrequency of her visits, consisted only of the estate agent and his assistant, and the two next-door neighbours, one beside her new home, the other round the corner, on the rear perimeter of the garden. They had seemed nice enough, and she supposed that people were the same just about everywhere. It was one's attitude to them, and theirs to you that really decided whether you sank or swam in a community. Then she nearly bit off her tongue at the inappropriateness of the wording of her last thought.

Silently chiding herself for being over-sensitive, she focused on the rear doors of the van, once more, and made her mind a blank for the next fifty miles. It was suddenly catapulted back to the present as she saw the van indicate to turn left. It pulled off up a slip-road towards a gathering of establishments that comprised a service stop with wide swathes of parking spaces, and a variety of eating places.

The removal men had had only a cup of tea from her this morning, and she presumed they were hungry and in need of a proper breakfast. She didn't feel in the least like eating, herself, but knew it would make good sense to put something in her belly, to give her some energy for dealing with the unloading and directing at the other end. Thus decided, she joined them in the queue for the till with a tray loaded with a full English breakfast, a pot of yoghurt, and a mug for tea.

She initially seated herself at a separate table, but was urged, before she had even sat down properly, to come and join the merry gang at a larger table at the rear of the dining area. Since their arrival the previous day, this small group of strangers had offered her a re-entry into human affairs, and she realised how much she appreciated it, when, on joining them, the 'head honcho' and owner of the van said that he had a bottle of champagne in his cab, to be cracked when all her possessions were in the new house.

He was of the opinion that all house moves should be celebrated as a moving on in life, and did this on a regular basis, unless he suspected that the couple were breaking up, or moving down-market due to financial problems. This gave her another reason to be glad that she had chosen this one-man-band to move her, and not one of the faceless large companies.

The last half of the journey passed without mishap, and it was only eleven o'clock when they pulled up outside number 45 Essex Road, in Market Darley. She had realised, about forty or fifty miles ago, how beautiful the countryside was becoming, and reached the town, from which she would commute to her job the three days of the week that she worked, with thoughts of appreciation of its architecture and surroundings.

It was an old market town, with a market cross and square, and many of its shops, if one raised one's eyes above display window level, clearly advertised their age. It looked like a place she could learn to forget and start life anew, and this made her smile, as the two vehicles in the tiny convoy pulled up outside her new home.

The rest of the day had been a whirlwind of activity for, although she was not involved in the unloading or transfer of her furniture and the boxes containing her smaller possessions, she was the one 'directing traffic', as it were. Yesterday afternoon, she had tried to keep abreast of the efficient and swift packing, to mark each box before it was loaded on to the van, but she had not managed to label them all, and she also wanted the furniture to go into the correct rooms while she had sufficient muscle to put it in place. Once they had gone, and she was on her own again, anything heavy in a wrong room would have to stay there until she had got to know someone with enough muscle-power to help her shift it to its correct position.

At lunchtime – about one-thirty, by choice of the removal men – she drove off to the local parade of shops which she had discovered on a previous visit, and bought enough fish and chips to feed them all, no matter how big their appetites proved to be. It was the least she could do, after all their friendly overtures to her, and she was saddened to think that she would never see those same faces again. They would just retreat into her past, after today, for they were not local, and would become just another memory, but a happy one this time.

Even her reception in the chip shop had been positive, with the man behind the counter, who turned out to be the owner, spotting a new face and asking her if she was just visiting – then wishing her the best of luck when she explained that she was only that day moving to the town.

When she arrived back with the food, the removal men had set up the dining table, attaching the top to the legs after its journey, had rooted out the dining chairs, and escorted her to what they had assumed (correctly) would be the dining room. They received their parcels of greasily steaming sustenance with suitable gestures of appreciation and gratitude, and set to, to make short work of her offerings.

As she scrunched up the empty papers to put in a black plastic bag from a roll she had, with forethought, brought with her in the car, she called out to see who wanted tea, and, after receiving a volley of affirmatives, entered the kitchen to find the kettle in pride of place, together with the box packed last, with mugs, tea, coffee, and sugar in it, waiting for her on the work surface. The milk, they had thoughtfully removed from the box in which it had been packed, and put into the newly brought-in and connected fridge.

After a flurry of, 'Left hand down a bit,' 'No, lift, not push,' 'Twist it so that we can get it through,' and 'Mind the doorframe, you donkey,' while the tea brewed, they came to collect their steaming mugs with gratitude, and not a little horse-play, more for her entertainment, she thought, than their own.

She had wondered if cold drinks would be more appropriate on an afternoon in August, but the British weather was behaving true to form, and a thick blanket of clouds hid the sky and smothered the heat of the sun, so it was quite a cool day, a good prod to her to check out the central heating system before autumn arrived, as it was likely to do, well before its traditional date, in this country.

The men had finally left at seven-thirty, wishing her good luck to a man, and waving frantically out of the cab window as the van drove away, an almost intimate part of her life for a day and a half, and she hadn't even known their names. And suddenly she was alone again, in a strange town where she had no friends or relatives, and just herself to bother about.

Chapter Two

<u>Friday 6th August, 2010 – evening and onwards</u>

Shaking herself back to the present, she began, slowly, to move from room to room, inspecting her new home with a critical eye. All in all, it was a good house, although just a bit too big for her on her own, but it was in good decorative order, if not to her taste, and it had been well maintained by its previous owners.

It had also been left immaculately clean and for this she was grateful. Her energy levels had been sapped and she no longer had the enthusiasm for the mundane jobs previously undertaken without thought. She considered that it was possible that she would be happy here, and looked forward to the time when this would be so, and she could feel like an ordinary person again.

Maybe she should get a dog or a cat, she wondered, just so that there was an extra heartbeat in the house, and something to talk to, so that she didn't feel as if she were going mad any more, when she talked to herself. A cat would be best, she decided, with her having to go to work three days a week. Dogs needed to be exercised, but a cat, although it walked to the beat of its own drum, could come and go as it pleased, with the addition of a cat flap, and would be an additional comfort to her on cold evenings, sitting on her lap and purring.

Oh! There was already a cat flap in the kitchen door, something she had not noted on any of her trips to view and measure up. Well, that was that decision made, then, and she determined to look in the Yellow Pages to try to locate a rescue centre from where she could choose a homeless animal to take in, and give the love and care it needed. Two waifs and strays together. What a team they would make!

Having ended her tour in the kitchen, having ascertained that all the bulky items of furniture were where they should be, she remembered that there had been a portion of chips, a saveloy, and a battered burger left at lunchtime, and she was glad she had not thrown them away. It was too late to look for shops open, and she was physically and emotionally exhausted from the rigours of the day. A few minutes on a plate in the microwave, and she could eat good old English comfort food, and go up to make up her bed for the night.

As she finished eating, however, there was a sharp rap at the front door, and she opened it to find the woman she had met previously, from the house next door, on her step. Introducing herself as Carole Winter, she extended an invitation to come round to her house for a glass of sherry.

Miriam was taking her first step into what was to be a period of whirling activity, as she was rapidly introduced by Mrs Winter, to the Women's Institute, where a young-for-her-years lady called Mabel Monaghan showed her their programme of events for the following autumn, and urged her to attend the special summer-break meetings. These were all talks by local people, about their particular interests, including local history, and the decline, rise and decline again, of agriculture in the surrounding area.

This sounded a good way to learn about where she was to make her new life, and she agreed, with alacrity, to attend the meetings, and join as soon as she was given the opportunity.

A meeting of the local book club, which this month was held at the home of a woman in her mid-thirties called Justine Cooper, introduced her to women a little closer to her own age, and she was fascinated that their list of books for the coming months included some quite racy titles.

She sat with them for two hours while they discussed the current volume under scrutiny, and found their impressions and insights intelligent and informative. Invited to the next meeting, she accepted immediately, and made a note of the book they were discussing earlier, so that she could get a copy, and add her own impressions to the general pot of opinions.

The ladies of the library, Liz and Becky, bade her a similar welcome to their world of literature, and provided her with a temporary ticket on the spot, informing her that she would receive her permanent ticket through the post, and telling her that they looked forward to seeing her again in the near future

In that first week, Carole was very dedicated, taking her to many other organisations, introducing her each time to the individual who ran it, and making her head spin with the plethora of new names she felt she needed to commit to memory. Mrs Winter seemed to know everyone in Market Darley, and so she should have done, having moved there from the north thirty-five years ago, on her marriage. She had lost almost all the accent that had identified her origins up until her move south.

Carole had also insisted on taking her to the local church on Sunday to meet the congregation, even introducing her to the members of the choir. The vicar welcomed her warmly to his parish, expressed the hope that she would become one of his flock, and join in with all the parish activities, which didn't seem impossible to Miriam, once she had met everyone that morning. His congregation was young, and the notice board in the entrance filled with notices of meetings, groups and social events. Maybe life would be kind to here, in this, her new start.

So busy and pleasant had her first days become in this new setting that she found herself, one evening, arranging a couple of vases of fresh flowers, one each to brighten up the dining and sitting rooms, and humming a tune as she cocked her head to one side to consider the balance of her arrangements. Without her realising it, she had moved from feeling numb to a sense of happiness and contentment, so long missing from her existence that she hardly recognised it.

Her commute to work was about the same as it had been from her old address, the transfer to another branch going without a hitch, and it seemed that life now held some promise for her. Her telephone started to ring with invitations from new friends, and her social life became almost as busy as it had been many years ago, when she had been young and carefree, and had no idea of the blow that life would one day deal her.

Carole Winter was an avid gardener, and began to help Miriam plan her own little piece of land. At the moment it was all laid to lawn, without a bed to break the runs of grass at front and back, and they began to go out to garden centres to see what was available for autumn planting, and what bulbs would go in in the autumn for the next spring.

Books from the library accelerated Miriam's interest in this hitherto unconsidered pastime, and she began to watch gardening programmes on the television, becoming hooked on the subject within a very short time. This, she considered, was because she had lived her life in limbo for so long. She could feel herself waking up, as if from a long hibernation, and it felt good to be part of everyday life again.

She also began to make friends at work, and sometimes spurned her usual home-coming train in favour of going out for a few drinks with colleagues from the office, returning home much later than usual, and feeling quite young again. Locally, she joined the reading group and attended a couple of meetings of the WI, as time-fillers, and found to her surprise that she enjoyed them, adding them to her list of regular outings. It seemed that, at last, she would be left in peace to lead as normal a life as she could, without all the hassle she had left behind when she had moved away.

She and Carole next door, who seemed to be relieved to spend a little time away from her husband, who was now retired, and whom she said got under her feet all the time, were happy to go into Market Darley on a Saturday afternoon to window shop and have a coffee and cake in the local coffee shop.

On Sunday mornings they walked to church together, even though Miriam had never been a regular church-goer in her life before. She even said her very first sincere prayer – one of thanks and gratitude that her nightmare seemed to be over, and that she was starting life anew.

On Sunday afternoons, Miriam drove while Carole sat in the passenger seat, and they toured round the various garden centres that seemed to surround the town, all of them hard to get to without a car. Carole had almost convinced her to dig a little vegetable patch, or even grow vegetables in pots, as there was nothing like food straight from garden to plate, she said.

It was on one such afternoon, just over a month since she had moved in, when they were discussing whether to go to all the trouble of turning over a patch of ground, or whether to use troughs, pots and planters for tomatoes, courgettes, strawberries and the like, and even maybe a plastic dustbin for new potatoes, that Miriam realised that she was doing most of the talking, and that Carole was uncharacteristically quiet.

'Are you OK?' she asked, wondering if maybe Carole and her husband had had a disagreement between the church service and now, or whether she just had a headache, or something similar, that was making her feel under par.

'I'm fine,' was the curt answer, and she lapsed back into a silence that soon became awkward for both of them.

'What is it?' Miriam risked another question, wondering if something she'd done had unintentionally upset her new friend.

'Nothing. You carry on with your plans,' her passenger replied, but there was the very slightest of chills in her voice, and the rest of the journey to the garden centre passed in silence.

Carole was equally distant as they walked around the area where packets of vegetable seeds were sold. She indicated, with a pointing finger, the varieties she recommended for container growing, hardly communicating at all, and leaving Miriam upset and mystified at what could have caused this sudden change in her previously very friendly neighbour.

Asking her brought forth nothing more than denial that there was anything wrong, and, in the end, Miriam suggested that they go back home early, without going on to a second establishment, because she had a headache – which wasn't a lie. The replacement of her normally irrepressible and ebullient friend by this uncommunicative and distant stranger had affected her considerably, and her temples were beginning to throb with pain.

Back home, Carole bade her a less than enthusiastic goodbye, with no comment that she would see her soon, and disappeared through her own front door without turning to wave, or thanking Miriam for the lift. Miriam entered her own house in considerable puzzlement. Her neighbour had seemed fine that morning at church, but by the afternoon, she had appeared not to be comfortable in her company any more. What on earth had she done?

Chapter Three

<u>Monday 13th September</u>

Miriam had not spoken to her neighbour again the day before, and left for work on Monday morning as confused as she had been the previous day. Her work and colleagues proved sufficient distraction during working hours, and she gladly forgot about this little glitch in her friendship with her neighbour. She agreed to go for a drink after work, partly because she knew she'd enjoy it, and partly because she was delaying going home; shelving the coolness that had so unexpectedly arisen between her and Carole.

Six of them went to the Jack of Three Sides, an old pub just off the town centre, situated on a small triangular island of land where the roads were unusually convoluted. It was an old building that had stayed in character, and to which she had never gone before.

The inside looked less contemporary than many of the public houses in the town where she now worked, and more like the establishment as it had existed many years ago. Every piece of wall was covered with pictures, framed sepia photographs and newspaper cuttings relating to the tiny area in which the pub stood. Pewter tankards hung from the beams, just below the very darkly nicotine-stained ceiling, and even this surface was not neglected, as some inventive soul had found a way to fasten pictures and paintings to the ceiling, so that even looking up was a delight.

The chairs and tables were, similarly, a mishmash of styles, but none of them new or out of place, and she stood at the bar just looking round in admiration at the fact that there was no dust. In a bar crammed with memories, there was nowhere one could see a plain surface, and yet everything was wonderfully clean.

Living near the station in Market Darley as she did, there was nothing to stop her having three glasses of wine, as she would not have to drive when she de-trained, and she thoroughly enjoyed herself that evening, sipping her chilled drinks, and gossiping with the others with whom she now shared her working life.

When her train finally arrived at her destination, it was much later than she usually arrived home, even after staying on for a drink, but she was relaxed and happy after the little boost of alcohol, and the bonhomie she had shared. It fleetingly crossed her mind to just dump her bags and knock on Carole's door and confront her, asking her outright how she seemed to have alienated her friend, but given the lateness of the hour, and the lovely relaxed feeling she was enjoying, she slid her key into the door, and dismissed the idea from her mind. A long, relaxing bath and then to bed with a book would round off the day very nicely, and she didn't want to spoil how she felt now with any bad-feeling.

That feeling evaporated completely when, picking up her mail from the hall carpet, she noticed that the top envelope had a very badly hand-written name, and no address, implying that it had been delivered by hand: and it was to Mrs Miriam Stourton, not Ms Darling.

Her hands immediately began to shake, and she sank down on to the carpet as her legs threatened to betray how she felt. No! Not here! Not again! she thought. It can't have followed me here! Letting go of the envelopes she held in her unsteady hand, she put her hands to her face, and began to sob. Her recent euphoria had completely evaporated with this one small discovery.

Monday 20th September

A steady flow of letters began to arrive, some in the naive hand of the first one, others in letters cut from newspapers and magazines. Some came in the post, others were dropped through her letterbox at night, and Miriam's newly minted self-confidence and happiness disappeared, from the receipt of that first missive.

Her applications to join various organisations were suddenly turned down, with no explanation given, invitations were withdrawn and, eventually, stopped being issued at all. Even at church, the previous morning, Carole had pleaded an upset stomach, and Miriam had found herself blanked and shunned by members of the congregation who had previously appeared friendly towards her. Even the vicar shook her hand very limply after the service, and moved on to the next person quickly, to rid himself of her company, it seemed to Miriam.

After a month of contentment and comparative happiness, within a week she had been reduced to a social pariah, and she knew it had started all over again, but this time she'd have to do something about it. She'd lived with it in her old home, but this time she was going to involve the police. She couldn't live the rest of her life constantly running away. She had to find a platform from which to plead her case, this time with the help and support, maybe even the protection, if things escalated, of the forces of law and order.

Detective Inspector Harry Falconer of the Market Darley CID was just scanning his diary for the week and exchanging morning pleasantries with his detective sergeant, 'Davey' Carmichael, when the telephone shrilled on his desk and, with a sigh of 'here we go again', he answered the call, holding up his free hand to stem the flow of Carmichael's enthusiastic conversation.

The woman on the other end of the line was almost hysterical, and it was a few minutes before he could calm her enough to be able to comprehend anything she said. She was obviously in a highly emotional state and, given that he had little in his diary for the day – and the state she was in, he decided, in the circumstances, that the situation merited a trip to her home, to interview her in privacy without the necessity of her making a trip to the police station.

'Come on, sunshine,' he cajoled his sergeant, as he ended the call. 'We've got a damsel in distress to rescue. Get your armour on, and we'll ride over to her tower and see what we can do for her.'

'What armour, sir? What tower? Ride? I don't know what you're talking about,' was his sergeant's reply.

'I know you don't, Carmichael, but that's about par for the course.'

'Why are you talking about golf now?'

'Come on, you. We've got the beginnings of a nasty case here. Make sure you've got your notebook, and I'll explain in the car on the way over. It's not far.'

'But where are we going? I don't underst ...' Carmichael's questions echoed all the way down the stairwell, as they made their way out of the station and into the car park.

Once safely strapped into Falconer's ritzy little Boxster, he began to relate what he had learned from the hysterical woman on the phone.

'Something's evidently happened in her life, in the past, that she's moved here to forget, but it seems that her story has followed her and caught up with her, and now she's receiving hate mail. I don't know any more details than that at the moment, but it sounded like she wasn't in a fit state to drive to the station, so I said we'd come to her. Somehow, although I don't have the whole story, this one doesn't feel like a storm in a teacup to me. It feels nasty.

'She says she's had abusive phone calls – numbers withheld, of course – silent phone calls in the middle of the night, and about seventy-odd letters, threatening her with all sorts of things. I don't know what happened yet, in her past, but it seems to have caused a furious reaction amongst those she's met and become friendly with, since she moved here.'

'She must be terrified, sir,' Carmichael commented, his brow furrowed with the effort to imagine his own wife in a similar situation.

'Well, she certainly sounded it on the phone.'

Chapter Four

<u>Monday 20th September</u>

When Falconer knocked smartly on the door of Miriam's house, there was a delay, during which they noticed the net curtains twitch, to establish who was calling, no doubt. Then there was the sound of bolts being drawn back and keys turned, before the front door opened just a crack, to the extent of its security chain, at which point they displayed their warrant cards to identify themselves.

The face that greeted them was blotchy and swollen, the eyes, as they surveyed their identification, red, and full of fear. In silence, the woman stood back and allowed the door to open just enough to admit them, before closing it again, and locking and bolting it behind them. Miriam Darling was still in her dressing gown, her hair tousled and wild, and she looked to be in the extremes of anxiety, as she preceded them into the living room.

The first thing that confronted them was a sofa completely covered in pieces of paper, some in scrawled childlike handwriting, others with cut-out letters to spell out their messages. There were dozens of the things, completely swamping the green leather surface, and Miriam simply looked at them, and then at her two visitors.

At that moment, the telephone rang, and, as she dragged herself across the room to answer it, Falconer looked at Carmichael, whose face was scrunched up in anger at this material evidence of hatred and spite.

She listened for a moment, then cried, 'Who are you? What do you want? Why don't you say something?' Her voice was shrill and harsh in the silence of the house. She slammed down the handset, pulling the plug from the wall in her impotent anger and frustration, then just wandered back to them, before collapsing into an armchair.

'What am I going to do?' she asked, in a voice hoarse with weeping. 'I can't keep on running. I've already gone back to my maiden name, but someone's found out. Am I never to be free of it? I haven't done anything wrong. It was just a tragic accident, and as if that wasn't enough, here I am being hounded again, like some sort of criminal.'

Falconer nodded at Carmichael and the letters. The sergeant, in complete silent understanding, donned a pair of latex gloves, and began collecting together the sheets of paper and putting them in evidence bags, to be checked later for fingerprints. The inspector took a seat in the armchair on the other side of the fireplace and gathered his reserves for interviewing this deeply distressed woman.

Miriam just sat in her chair, her hands in her lap, her head drooping, like a marionette that had had all its strings cut. She was evidently steeling herself, too, for the ordeal to come.

His task swiftly completed, Carmichael sank down on the now unencumbered sofa and removed his notepad from his pocket, ready to record what the woman had to say. He waited in silence for Falconer to commence his questioning.

'I'd like you to tell me what it is in your past that has 'followed' you here, and why the reaction is so extreme. There's no need to rush. Just tell it in your own time, so that we can understand what has been happening to you recently,' he said, his voice quiet and almost tender.

'It was something that happened just over a year ago.' Miriam's voice was so low, they could hardly catch what she was saying, but after clearing her throat and shaking her head, she continued at a more easily discernible volume.

'One year, one month, and six days ago, to be precise – I can't seem to stop counting the time that has elapsed. I was married then, and we had a son. Mark, my husband's name was, and Ben was our son, only four years old, and full of life.' Here she had to break off, as her voice cracked, and tears began to track down her cheeks.

'My parents moved to Spain three years ago, when Dad took early retirement, so we went out to visit them in the summer, and at Christmas. Although it was rather expensive, it was cheaper than taking a break through a travel agent, and it meant that at least they saw their grandson twice a year. We used Skype, of course, but Mum wanted to cuddle Ben, and Dad wanted to take him to the beach and play football and all those sort of grandfatherly things.

'It was when we went out last summer that *it* happened, and my nightmare began, although I didn't realise people were so cruel, and it would go on for so long that I wouldn't have time to come to terms with it in peace, and mourn them in privacy.'

'What was *it*?' asked Falconer, feeling that they weren't really getting anywhere, and he needed to get to the nub of the matter, and discover the details of the mystery event.

'We had planned to go along the coast to a little cove that was very beautiful, but usually completely empty of holiday-makers. Ben was excited at the thought of getting a bit of beach to himself, so that he could make his sandcastles without a game of football being played through his efforts, and people's dogs arriving to dig in his turrets.

'I suggested that we walk along the cliffs to get to it, as there was a rudimentary set of steps there, although they were difficult to descend, having been cut out of the cliffs, but Mark had very different ideas. He'd been a bit scratchy that holiday, and I didn't want another argument – we'd already had quite a few blow-ups, and I knew he was fed up to the back teeth of always going to the same place, and having to stay with my parents.

'I was determined that we wouldn't fall out that day, and that maybe the deserted cove would work its magic on him, and put him in a good mood for once. How naive I was; and how little foresight I managed to display, when you consider the outcome.'

Carmichael was scribbling like fury, but found a second or two to look at the inspector, and roll his eyes at the prolonged explanation of what had happened; that event still seeming a long way away, buried in this miasma of memories, as it was. Falconer acknowledged his partner's rolling eyes by pulling a face in reply. Miriam Darling sat with her head down, twisting her fingers together in her lap, lost in the past.

'So, what actually happened when you got to the beach?'

'Oh, Mark insisted that we go to the main beach and hire a little boat. He said that would be a much more picturesque way of approaching the cove, and would mean we didn't have to risk the old steps down from the cliff top.

'I wasn't sure, not knowing what the water was like round the slight headland, and disagreed, saying that we could take the utmost care on the steps, and pointed out to him that unknown waters could be dangerous. That was when we had our little row – the one I'd been desperate to avoid – with hordes of witnesses. In the end, I said I didn't want to go, if Mark insisted on hiring a boat.

'That was like a red rag to a bull for him, and he took Ben's hand and stomped off towards the man who rented out the small craft. I just stood by, feeling helpless as usual, but supposing that everything would turn out all right in the end, and thinking Mark might even be in a good mood if he got his own way on this one. If only, just that once, I hadn't played the part of the compliant wife!

'And so we set off. It really was a small boat – a wooden one. Do they call those little things 'clinker-built'? – and Mark, of course, took charge of the oars, being the man of the family. It seemed a perfectly charming way to reach our destination at first, but, as we rounded the headland, the going got more difficult, and Mark started to struggle to keep control of the little boat.

'When I realised he was in difficulties, I offered to take a turn on one of the oars, so that we could row together, and double our power to fight the current, but he would have none of that. He was always stubborn, and hated to fail at anything. At that point, this was a test of his manhood, in his mind, and he struggled on, but the further we disappeared from sight of the busy beach, the more unruly the sea became.

'That was when I got really frightened, and told him he ought to turn back, as the sea was getting far too rough. The wind had got up, too, and we were rolling all over the place, with the waves breaking over the boat and swamping us. Ben was crying and I was holding him, trying to comfort him, and telling him that Daddy would soon get us back to the nice beach where he always played.

'That was the last coherent thought I had. There was a gust of wind, and a particularly large wave engulfed our tiny boat, and it capsized, throwing the three of us, plunging, into the roughness of the sea.

'There were incredibly strong currents there, and all I could think of was to catch hold of the underside of the boat and scream for help, although I knew my cries would be blown away by the wind. By the time I had a firm hold of it, I looked round, and both Mark and Ben were gone. That's when I really started screaming. I hadn't realised how one's life could be turned upside down in just a couple of seconds, the status quo irretrievably lost, the future completely blank and needing to be rewritten.

'I was the lucky one. Someone on the top of the headland, looking at the seabirds swirling around the inshore waters, happened to catch sight of my precarious situation, he alerted the coastguard – and I was rescued.'

Miriam paused here, to gather her strength for the end of the tragic tale. 'Mark's and Ben's bodies were washed ashore further along the coastline two days later; and my life effectively ended. I might as well have drowned with them. I feel like I'm already dead and suffering in hell, with all that's happened since, and now it's happening all over again.'

'And all the sorts of things that have occurred here, happened where you used to live?'

'Live? Huh! Existed, more like. But, yes, I was held in custody in Spain by the police. People remembered, you see, how we'd argued on the beach. My mother's neighbours remembered how we'd argued at her house – those villas are jerry-built, and the sound-proofing is non-existent. They thought I'd pushed them out of the boat, and that was the reason it capsized. I was cast in the role of a murdering wife and mother.

'I can't speak Spanish, and neither can my parents beyond a few words of greeting and 'please' and 'thank you', and I was dazed with my loss, and bewildered as to what was going on around me. It was a complete nightmare. There I was, locked away from the only comfort available to me – my parents – and I didn't understand a word of what was being said to me.

'Of course, eventually they brought in an interpreter, but it was a resort mainly for the Spanish themselves, and the interpreter, although she could speak some English, could not understand what I was saying, and seemed to make up her own mind as to what I had told her.'

'So what set off this toxic gossip, then?' asked Falconer, still pursuing his fox, but feeling that the further he moved forward the further away he was from his quarry.

'It started with the Spanish press. It was quiet in the journalistic world, it being holiday time; they seized my tragedy as a terrier seizes a rat, and I made the front page, painted as black as night. Just to add to my misfortunes, there was an English journalist on holiday about fifty kilometres away. He saw the story and descended on my parents and their neighbours like a wolf on the fold.

'He couldn't get to see me, but he did trace several people who had been on the beach that day – isn't it ironic that he spoke the lingo? Of course, he phoned it in, and started the same hare running in the English press. By the time I got back, I was branded as a murderess, and nothing I could say would change that, even though the Spanish police had traced someone on a fishing boat who had actually seen us capsize.

'I was harassed in my home by journalists. I started receiving anonymous threatening letters and silent phone calls, just like now. My car had paint-stripper thrown over it, people I'd known all my life, shunned me in the street. Some of them even spat at me, and one joker poured weedkiller over my front lawn one night, to spell out 'murderer'. That's when I knew what it was to be in hell.

'I took all the precautions I could to get away from it all. I moved to a rented property fifty miles away, adopting my maiden name, dying my hair and having it cut really short. I changed the way I dressed, and started not wearing make-up – anything so that I was not connected to what had befallen my family on that dreadful holiday.

'Eventually I moved here, and I seemed to have made a really solid start on a new and normal life. Carole Winter next door befriended me and introduced me to a host of people and organisations where I was made to feel really welcome. I'd applied to join the WI, I'd been invited to join a book club, I'd met the ladies of the church, the choir and the library, and Carole, who is a keen gardener, was helping me plan my little plot out at the back. Sundays were fun. We used to go to the service together, then go off in my car and stroll round the garden centres, looking for bulbs, seeds and plants that would be suitable for what had become my new hobby: gardening.

'Then, one day, she just 'cut' me: 'blanked' me as if she had never met me before. I found I was *persona non grata* wherever I went, and then it just started all over again. I don't know who made the connection, or why they passed it on, but I'm right back to square one, and now there's nowhere else to go,' she concluded on a mournful note.

'You *have* been through the mill, haven't you? Let me think a while and see what I can come up with. Do you work outside the home at all?'

'Yes. I work for a bank – Mondays, Wednesdays, and Fridays.'

'And has there been any trouble there?'

'Not so far, but I commute, and mix with a totally different set of people there. It's the only part of my life with some sanity left in it, the only place where I get treated like a normal human being. I'm not giving that up,' she stated in a firmer voice.

'OK. For now,' Falconer replied, 'what I can do is have a patrol car pass your house when you're at home, to make sure there's no physical attack on you, and put one of the uniformed constables to patrol this area, giving us a man on the ground.

'In the meantime you're going to have to consider changing your identity completely, perhaps disappear into the anonymity of a large city. Market Darley's fairly small, and people are nosier about their neighbours than they are in the sprawling confusion of a city.'

'I see your point,' she agreed. 'I do exactly as I planned before, but become the needle in a much bigger haystack.'

'Spot on! Now, I'll give you my card, and I'll write my home number on the back, so that you can get hold of me anytime. I hate bullying, especially the cowardly, anonymous kind, and when it's completely unfounded, it really gets my goat,' the inspector growled with great sincerity. 'There it is. Any time, day or night! And I mean that! I don't live far away – in fact I'm closer to you than I am to the police station, and I can be here in a few minutes, and alert the boys in blue on my way.

'In the meantime, may I suggest that when you are here you keep away from the windows. I know you've got net curtains and I don't want to frighten you, but I also don't want you to make yourself an unwitting target for some nutter.'

'Thank you for taking me so seriously,' she murmured, as she saw them out of the front door, opening it only wide enough to allow them to squeeze through it, and they heard her lock and bolt it again, as she had when they arrived.

Chapter Five

<u>Tuesday 21st September</u>

Falconer's home phone rang shrilly at just after half-past six that morning, rousing him from a light doze in which he dreamt of a woman he had glimpsed, briefly but devastatingly, earlier that year. She had skin the colour of ebony and was, in his opinion, the most beautiful woman he had ever set eyes on.

Things were going well in the dream, and they were sipping cocktails at some function or other, when the trilling of the telephone began to break up the conviviality of the occasion. As if a herald of the bad news that was to come in his dream, his old Nanny Vogel approached the bar, stopped by his side, and gave him her cruel and knowing smile, while the attractive woman, Dr Dubois, turned into a pillar of smoke and began to disperse.

Arriving suddenly to full wakefulness, he felt both cheated and disturbed as he reached for the handset beside his bed, answering it with an uncharacteristically blunt 'Yes?'

'Is that you, Inspector Falconer,' a distressed and tearful voice enquired. 'Only things have got worse.'

Recognising Miriam Darling's voice immediately, he pulled himself together, to treat her with a more professional attitude, even if he was in his pyjamas and lying in bed. These things mattered! 'What's happened now?' he asked her gently, hoping she hadn't been injured.

'I got a brick through my front window yesterday – well, during the night, actually – but as the curtains were drawn, it didn't really do any damage, but when I opened the door to take in the milk this morning, someone had sprayed 'killer' on my front door in black paint. I simply don't know what to do. Please help me, Inspector. I'm at my wits' end.'

'I'll get an officer over to take samples of the paint, and he'll take away the brick as evidence, although there's little likelihood it will offer anything useful as to who threw it. I'll get that organised, and I'll be with you in less than an hour to take another statement. I'll also arrange for a female PC to be billeted with you, as I seem to remember that you don't work on a Tuesday.'

'That's very kind of you, Inspector. I shall feel a lot safer for seeing you again, and a PC in the house will be a great relief. At least I'll have a witness to anything else that happens, and an ally, if I need physical help.' She sounded calmer already, and Falconer was pleased with his idea of having a PC in residence. If the officer herself made her presence known, maybe it would act as a deterrent.

'I'll be with you as soon as I can, Ms Darling, and I'll get on the phone straight after this call and set the wheels in motion for a SOCO officer and a PC to be dispatched.'

As soon as he ended the call, he rang the station with a cheery, 'Hello, Bob. How's tricks?' only to find that Bob Bryant – *Bob Bryant* – had taken a *day's leave*, and he was talking to PC Barry Sugden, more usually to be found booking in 'guests' in the custody suite.

'Sorry about that,' he apologised, 'only it always *is* Bob Bryant, so I simply wasn't prepared to find someone else answering the phone.'

'Don't apologise, sir – everyone else has said the same thing. I've just told them that, as one of the Immortals, Bob sometimes has to report to the planet Zog on what he has discovered in his current role, and then he'll get his transfer to another location round about the year 2073. Nobody's questioned my answer yet, but for your personal information, he's going to have a tooth out, and wants to slink back home and suffer in peace, but don't tell anyone else. The new boys, in particular, will be devastated, if they find out the reason for his day away from the station is such a mundane affair.'

Falconer knew only too well the web of bantering fantasy that existed between the younger members of the uniformed branch about the ever-present desk sergeant who, it was rumoured by these junior members of the force, had been there from the beginning of time, and would remain there, as an Immortal, until the end of the universe.

'Look, Barry, I need someone to come out to scout for evidence at the site of what I can only describe as a 'hate crime', and I need a PC – get me Starr if you can – to join me here.' After a little more explanation and giving the address, he hung up and got ready as speedily as he could, to visit Miriam Darling again. He could only imagine her distress and fear, and wanted to do what he could to reassure her as quickly as possible.

He arrived there less than half an hour after her distress call. When the door was opened by an even smaller crack than it had been on his last visit, he looked straight at her face, and, on gaining admittance, saw that she was already petrified with the escalation of events. He sat with her, giving what comfort he could, until PC Starr arrived and distracted her by asking to show the policewoman where everything was in the kitchen, so that she should be familiar with everything she needed to make tea, coffee and sandwiches.

Falconer left the two of them in the kitchen, opening and closing cupboard doors. Miriam seemed distracted enough to carry out this simple task; evidently feeling more confident now she had someone with her for the day.

Back at the station, he found that no activity in the immediate vicinity of the address had been reported by either foot patrol or passing patrol cars, and cudgelled his brain at how to get at the root of this spiteful behaviour. The neighbours were an obvious starting point, but he felt that they would be better left until Miriam went to work tomorrow, so that they would have had time to cool off, after being questioned, before she returned home from work.

Falconer got another early reveille the next morning – this time at 6.10, and from the familiar but unusually muffled voice of Bob Bryant; he must still have cotton wool in his mouth after his extraction the day before. Without preamble, the sergeant went straight into his story. 'One of yours, I believe, Harry. A Ms Darling. Been receiving hate mail, nasty phone calls and a brick through the window.'

When Falconer confirmed that this was his baby, the sergeant continued, 'Well, she's had another faceless visitor. Apparently she came down this morning at half-past five because she couldn't sleep, and decided a cup of tea would be a good thing. She hadn't had any more phone calls and was feeling quite cheerful, she said, when she started off down the stairs.

'That was when she smelled it. Someone had inserted a substantial amount of dog-shit through her letterbox, and then thrown the accompanying note, to land it clear of the first offering.'

'Nasty!' was the inspector's only comment.

'Quite!' countered the desk sergeant. 'But the note was much worse. It informed her that the next time it would be petrol-soaked rags, and that the author of the note always carried a box of matches or a lighter, so that he was never short of a flame. He then ended it by referring to her as a murdering bitch who wasn't going to get away with it, even if the law couldn't touch her.'

'I'm on my way, Bob, see if I can catch her before she leaves for work. Have we got anywhere we could use as a safe house for her at short notice? It would only be until she can find something to rent well away from here.'

'I'll see what I can do,' Bob assured him, and ended the call.

Miriam Darling was getting ready to leave for work when Falconer arrived, no longer shaking and crying, but showing a cold, hard side to her character that he had not seen before.

Allowing him a brief fifteen minutes, the most she could, to keep herself on schedule for catching her usual train, she sat down with him in the living room and listened to his suggestion about her moving temporarily to a safe house. Once she had chosen somewhere else to live, if she so desired, he could inform the local police station of her background, and get them to keep a discreet eye on her.

'I don't think that will be necessary, Inspector, although I'm very grateful for what you've done for me, but I think it's time for me to plough my own furrow now, don't you?'

He left her home that day more puzzled than reassured, and feeling that she was being blasé about the escalating danger to her, but there was nothing he could do about it. He could only provide the help and protection that he thought she needed if she was willing to accept it, and she'd been unbelievably distant when she'd spoken to him; almost as if she'd been a different person.

He didn't bother going home again, as it simply wasn't worth the extra to-ing and fro-ing, and seven thirty saw him behind his desk sorting through the paperwork that had accumulated since he had last sat there, and mulling over what had been happening in Ms Darling's life over the past couple of weeks.

It was the telephone that disturbed his reverie, but what an interruption it proved to be. PC Merv Green had been on duty in and around the railway station that morning, keeping an eye on vehicles in the station car park, and walking round the station periodically to make sure that there wasn't a pickpocket at work. Cities didn't have a monopoly on petty crime like this. It happened in relatively small places too.

He had been making his way along one of the platforms where the usually jostling crowd of commuters was waiting for the arrival of their morning train, all trying to be in a position to get into a compartment first and bag the best – or maybe the only – seat. As the train approached the station, there had been a yell from the furthest end of the platform, and cries went up: 'Woman under the train!' 'Someone pushed her! I saw!' 'I never saw her jump!' 'Get an ambulance!' and from one anonymous wag: 'Get a bucket and shovel!'

Green ran, pushing people out of his way in his anxiety to confirm what he had heard shouted; and they weren't wrong. The train was not so long that it still covered what was left of whoever had gone under it, and Green came perilously close to losing the contents of his stomach, just avoiding an unexpected rebate on his breakfast.

When Green called it in, although he had no name for the victim, or even confirmation of the sex, Bob Bryant had a gut feeling that this one was for Falconer, and called it through to him.

The inspector's response was unusually coarse and unexpectedly heartfelt: 'No! No! No, no, no! Damn! Damn it! No! Oh, shit! Bugger!' he yelled, to himself, rather than to Bob Bryant on the other end of the line. 'I should have waited, and escorted her to the train this morning, after what happened during the night. Bugger! Arse! What a negligent fool I am!'

'If it's her, Harry, it's hardly your fault, is it?' asked Bob Bryant, trying to dispel Falconer's feelings of guilt and anguish.

'But the threat in that last letter was chilling, and we should – *I should* – have taken it more seriously. That wasn't just a case of name-calling; that was a threat to her life, and even *I* didn't take it seriously enough. I suppose I thought that her tormentor would only act on his evil impulses when she was in her own home. Why didn't I consider her safety in going to work, or rather the danger she was in when she was in transit? I'm an absolute fool!'

'I should get yourself down to the railway station, and make sure it's her first, before you start beating your breast and tearing out your hair,' was the calm advice of the desk sergeant. Falconer took it at its worth, and calmed himself with difficulty while preparing to go to see the remains.

When he arrived at the railway station and sought out the correct platform, he realised what a good job Green had done. The man had used his loaf, and requested that the train be moved as far as it could along the track, allowing a clear view of where the victim had landed, getting those who were alighting at Market Darley to use the far exit, so as not to contaminate what must now be considered a crime scene.

The passengers waiting to board had been crowded into the station's waiting room, and were now waiting to be interviewed, bleating like sheep at how late they would be for work, meetings and the like, while yelling into their respective mobile phones trying to 'big up' what they were now declaring to be a bloody nuisance. But perhaps secretly believing that the morning's experience would be something that they could dine out on for months.

The area of platform itself had been isolated with blue-and-white crime tape, which now fluttered in the slightly chilly September breeze. Thus was the situation when Falconer arrived, in the sure and certain knowledge that Carmichael was not far behind him. That was cold comfort, however, as he felt he should have been able to save this poor, persecuted woman from having to pay the ultimate price for what was, in fact, an accident, blown out of all proportion and sensationalised by the press.

After Carmichael arrived, his face a woeful mask, it took the two of them an hour and a half to gather all the names, addresses and telephone numbers of the daily commuters, leaving them to reassemble at the far end of the platform in anticipation of the next train, all chattering like starlings about this unexpected interruption to their usual boring daily schedule.

There were already white-suited officers at work where the commuter had gone under the train: Falconer was able to give an adequate identification from scraps of torn clothing that had matched what she was wearing when he had visited her before she left for the station, but there was nothing really for them to find. What evidence does a little push leave? What trace could there be of the little shove, that just tips a person's balance, and causes them to fall?

Although all the other would-be passengers on that train would need to be interviewed, to see if anyone owned up to standing close enough to Miriam Darling to have witnessed whether she propelled herself in front of that train, or whether she was given a helping hand, it was a job they would leave to the uniformed branch. They would try to uncover the network of rumour and lies that had made Miriam's life such a misery before today, hoping against hope that they would be able to trace it to its original source in the town, but it would be a thankless task, and one unlikely to be successfully concluded.

Falconer finally left feeling very downhearted, and Carmichael had a glum expression that clearly indicated his feeling that they were facing a hopeless task. 'I don't know who is responsible for what that poor woman went through,' commented Falconer as they arrived back at their cars, 'but they might as well have handed her a chalice of poison and bade her drink it, for the outcome would have been the same.'

Chapter Six

Wednesday 22nd September

Falconer and Carmichael had spent the previous afternoon clearing their desks as best as they could to give them a free run at the new case, and had decided to start their investigations with the neighbours. Rumour and gossip usually emanated from someone close to the 'target' and, as Miriam had not lived in the area long, they had decided to start with those who had been physically close to her.

Their first visit was to Carole Winter, whom Falconer knew had befriended her new neighbour. If not involved herself, maybe she could give them some leads as to whom she had introduced Miriam to.

Carole's face 'closed' when she saw who was at her door, and they were invited inside reluctantly, her face bearing an icy smile that did not touch her eyes.

After introducing themselves, Falconer explained why they were there, although he had little doubt that she had realised that as soon as they had displayed their warrant cards.

'I was good to that girl,' she spat at them, defensively. 'I toted her around everywhere with me, introducing her to everyone I know, and then I found out what she had done – and not even a whisper to me that she had a past.' Mrs Winter sat bolt upright in an armchair, her hands clasped in her lap, a look of defiance on her face.

'She'd lied to me by her silence, and I wasn't having that – not having found out what she'd done and got away with.'

'Who told you?' asked Falconer, keeping his question as brief as possible so as not to prompt the flow of indignation and self-righteousness often found in some church-goers who would happily 'cast the first stone', and considered that they themselves were incapable of sin.

'It was Liz from the library. If she's bored, when the library's not busy, she amuses herself by 'Googling' new ticket-holders. The poor girl got much more than she bargained for when she searched for Miriam Stourton, nee Darling. And, before you ask, the application form to join the library service has a lot of seemingly irrelevant questions on it, including maiden name, and she had inadvertently put her married name in that space.

'Well, that really set the cat among the pigeons, and we had a long talk about what to do. It was Liz's suggestion – that's Elizabeth Beckett – that we spread the word that the woman was a danger to society. She should've been locked away, and the key thrown over a cliff. What a wicked deed, to kill her husband and her own child like that! She deserved to burn in hell, and I hope she is doing just that, now.'

'Crikey!' Carmichael later exclaimed. They'd certainly stirred up a hornets' nest of resentment at this house.

'Can you give me the names of the other people to whom you introduced Ms Darling?' asked Falconer, thinking to get a head start, but he'd stirred up another spurt of contumely.

'Darling, my bum! She was no more *Ms Darling* than I am the Aga Khan! Darling, my big fat hairy arse! But I'll answer your question, and then I want you out of this house. This has been a shocking time for me, ending up with a murderer living next door, and I want to forget it as quickly as possible, and get back to my normal tranquil life. What a good actress that woman was! I'd never have guessed she had such evil in her heart!'

The rest of the interviews conducted, from the names Mrs Winter provided, were either full of the same contempt, or with a holier-than-thou attitude that made Falconer's stomach turn.

Elizabeth Beckett at the library merely displayed astonishment that she could have uncovered such duplicity, but her colleague, Becky Troughton, claimed that she had taken an instant dislike to the woman, and that she had felt from the first that there was something wrong with her. How some people strive to find something a little bit 'special' about themselves, some supernatural ability that sets them apart from others! Falconer felt that this was the case here. Had the information never become public knowledge, Ms Troughton would probably be saying that she had sensed a good soul in Miriam Darling, and had taken to her at their very first meeting. Feelings, schmeelings! he thought in disgust.

At the church, although he spoke to the incumbent, a selection of the ladies of the congregation and choir, it was the holier-than-thou, pious attitude he encountered, many offering to pray for her forgiveness, yet none who believed in her innocence, and absolutely no one who would admit to making silent phone calls or sending anonymous letters. What an upright slice of society all these people seemed to form, and yet he had counted at least seventy letters on Miriam Darling's sofa the first time he had gone to her house.

Mabel Monaghan, the head honcho at the WI, was highly indignant that such a woman should even have considered joining the organisation, and admitted that she had torn up Miriam's application as soon as she had heard about her murky past.

'And you believed it without question?' Falconer had asked her.

'There is no fire without some smoke,' she had replied, getting the quotation right where so many others mangled it.

The only positive response he got was from Justine Cooper, the nominal leader of the book club that met once a month. 'I'd thought of asking her to give us a talk about her ordeal, so that we could, maybe, find a few literary similarities with this sort of persecution, and choose our next book along those lines,' she had admitted, when questioned.

'I suppose it was a rather morbid thought, though, given what she was going through, and for the second time. And now she's dead! Still, every cloud has a silver lining. We could still discuss her situation at our next meeting, and go ahead with that as a theme without her actually being there.' Now there was a hard-faced young woman, Falconer thought, as they left her house. She should have been a journalist, the way she seized things and twisted them to her ultimate advantage.

'I don't like these people.' Carmichael, as usual, summed up his feeling succinctly. 'I don't think I've ever met such a bunch of two-faced, trouble-making people who aren't actually criminals.'

'I'm with you on that one, Carmichael,' agreed Falconer, and then noticed that his sergeant had his pen in his mouth again – a habit of which he thought he had broken him.

'Put out your tongue, Sergeant,' he ordered, at the kerb-side, in public.

Looking a mite embarrassed, Carmichael removed the ballpoint pen from his mouth and complied.

'As I thought! The colour of an aubergine! When we get back to the station, go straight to the canteen and see if you can get them to serve you up a cup of coffee from the very dregs of the urn. That's the only thing we've found that seems to strip the ink.'

'Yes, sir,' agreed Carmichael, glumly.

Nothing was gleaned from the uniformed staff who had spent the hours after the return of the commuters trailing around the addresses given at the station that morning. Oh, yes, they'd come across a few who admitted to standing near, but not directly behind, Miriam Darling, but none that would admit to having pushed, or even accidentally nudged her, and no one had seen anything to which they were willing to admit.

With a heavy heart, Falconer knew that all the officers involved would just have to start all over again, and see if they couldn't coax a reluctant memory from someone, even if not an admission of guilt, but it was going to be a long and tedious job, and he still felt himself responsible for what had happened. What had possessed him, leaving her to make her own way to the railway station? He should have accompanied her. He had been negligent, and a sorely put-upon, innocent woman had paid for his lack of forethought with her life.

If only he had advised her not to go to work until she had been installed in a safe house. If! If! If only he had driven her to the station and waited with her. He would have kept her well away from the edge of the platform and, maybe, by the time she had returned to Market Darley that evening, he could have met her from the train with the address of a safe house into which she could move with immediate effect.

The week after Miriam Darling had been mangled by an incoming train was a week of reflection, regret and soul-searching for the inspector, and he was in an unusually glum mood when he picked up a white envelope from his post, one morning and slit it open, to find it was from Miriam Darling's bank manager, and had a smaller envelope enclosed with it, marked with his name.

'Well, I'll be blowed!' he exclaimed. 'What on earth can this be?'

'This' was a letter from her bank, explaining that the enclosed envelope had been handed to the manager by Miriam Darling herself, with the instructions that it was to be kept there in safe keeping, and only sent, in the event of her death, and even then not until a week had elapsed.

'Curiouser and curiouser,' quoted Falconer, as he slit open the second and smaller envelope. Inside, he found a letter, handwritten, explaining everything, and which saddened him even more than he would have thought it could. He read:

Dear Inspector Falconer,

> *I apologise for all the work I must have caused you and your colleagues over the last seven days, and now is the time for explanations. If, as I have planned, I have gone under a train at the local station, then my intentions will have gone as I hoped, and I shall be dead.*

> *I knew I couldn't face starting yet another life, because I think my past will follow me to the ends of the earth, given the information technology available today, so I have decided to join my husband and son 'on the other side'.*

> *I didn't want to leave this life without a little bit of revenge on those who had tormented me, so I will have made my death look as much like murder as I can, and have left it for you to suspect and question those who tormented me, and I hope they are made to feel hellishly uncomfortable.*

> *My last hope is that, with the delivery of my letter to you, the truth will be made public, so that they can feel the guilt they share in my carrying out of this act of self-destruction. I don't wish to carry on as things are, and I hope that what I did will give them cause to think, next time they are in receipt of a juicy*

piece of gossip, and maybe hold back, when they are tempted to pass it on.

Many thanks for your help and support, and to your colleagues who did their best to keep me safe,

Miriam Stourton, nee Darling

Falconer's throat was almost closed with emotion as he finished reading and, putting the letter on Carmichael's desk, in full view, where he would find it as soon as he sat down, he left the office and went for a walk in the clean, clear air of a beautiful September morning.

THE END

[1] *See* Christmas Mourning

Also by Andrea Frazer

The Belchester Chronicles
Strangeways To Oldham
White Christmas with a Wobbly Knee
Snowballs and Scotch Mist
Old Moorhen's Shredded Sporran
Caribbean Sunset with a Yellow Parrot

The Falconer Files - Brief Cases
Love Me to Death
A Sidecar Named Expire
Battered To Death
Toxic Gossip
Driven To It
All Hallows
Written Out
Death of a Pantomime Cow
The Complete Falconer Files Brief Cases Books 1 - 8

The Falconer Files Brief Cases Collections
The Falconer Files Brief Cases Books 1 - 4

The Falconer Files Brief Cases Books 5 - 8

The Falconer Files Collections
The Falconer Files Murder Mysteries Books 1 - 3
The Falconer Files Murder Mysteries Books 4 - 6
The Falconer Files Murder Mysteries Books 7 - 9
The Falconer Files Murder Mysteries Books 10 - 14
The Falconer Files Murder Mysteries Books 8 - 14
The Falconer Files Murder Mysteries Books 1 - 7

The Falconer Files Murder Mysteries
Death of an Old Git
Choked Off
Inkier than the Sword
Pascal Passion
Murder at The Manse
Music to Die For
Strict and Peculiar
Christmas Mourning
Grave Stones
Death in High Circles
Glass House
Bells and Smells
Shadows and Sins
Nuptial Sacrifice

The Fine Line
High-Wired

Tight Rope

Standalone
Choral Mayhem
Down and Dirty in the Dordogne
The Curious Case of the Black Swan Song
A Fresh of Breath Air
God Rob Ye Merry Gentlemen
The Bookcase of Sherman Holmes
The Complete Falconer Files Murder Mysteries Books 1 - 14
Down and Dirty in der Dordogne
Christmas Box Set
The Belchester Chronicles Books 1 - 3
Murder and Mayhem